A VIRGIN'S DIARY

David Wilbourne was born in Derbyshire, grew up in Yorkshire, studied in Cambridge and then returned to Yorkshire as a parish priest. He served in parishes in Middlesbrough and near Pontefract, before being appointed Archbishop of York's chaplain and Director of Ordinands. Since 1997 he has been vicar of the moors' market town of Helmsley.

Like *A Virgin's Diary*, his previous publications combine poignancy and humour and include *Archbishop's Diary* (SPCK 1995) and *A Vicar's Diary* (HarperCollins 1998).

He is married to Rachel, a history teacher, and they have three daughters.

ACKNOWLEDGEMENTS

Once again, I am indebted to my wife, Rachel, for encouraging, editing and proof-reading this work, as she has done with all my other writing.

I am grateful to *SeeN*, the magazine of the York Diocese, for publishing four short pieces I had written, which then generated the idea for this book.

Alison Barr, the commissioning editor at SPCK, has been a delight to work with. Her helpful suggestions, coupled with a speedy and efficient management of the project, make her stand out as exemplary among editors.

A
VIRGIN'S
DIARY

DAVID WILBOURNE

Azure
1 Marylebone Road
London
NW1 4DU

Copyright © David Wilbourne 1999

All rights reserved. No part of this book may be
reproduced or transmitted in any form or by any means,
electronic or mechanical, including photocopying, recording,
or by any information storage and retrieval system, without
permission in writing from the
publisher.

British Library Cataloguing-in-Publication Data

A catalogue record of this book is available from
the British Library

ISBN 190269 403 1

Typeset by Pioneer Associates, Perthshire
Printed in Great Britain by
Caledonian International Ltd, Glasgow

Contents

For Rachel

For two millennia of Christian history,
the Virgin Mary
has popped up in visions throughout the world:
Lourdes, Walsingham, Knock, Basingstoke . . .
How all this time travel
affected a quirky adolescent Palestinian girl,
already bewildered by a peculiar conception,
is recorded
in this recently discovered diary
of her pregnant months.

~ *Part One* ~

~ Friday 26 March ~

I've read them all. I've been smug with Samuel Pepys, I've been portly with Parson Woodforde, I've frolicked with Francis Kilvert, I've agonized with Anne Frank, I've been politically acute with Anthony Crosland, I've been adolescent with Adrian Mole, I've been bold with Bridget Jones . . . But no other diary starts like mine. I've been up all night, being violently sick – sick over the bedding, sick over the garden, sick over the well, sick over the vellum on which I'm trying to write this first diary entry. It's a good thing that vellum is reasonably wipe-clean.

Why all this sickness? It could be Momma's pizza. She's been getting into an experimental mood recently. The peach, pomegranate and St Peter's fish concoction she came up with yesterday struck me as odd at the time. Certainly not the taste to storm the new age that everyone's getting so excited about these days.

Or it could be pregnancy sickness, which seems a bit unfair since it was only yesterday I was diagnosed positive. It might have waited a week or two.

~ Saturday 27 March ~

The Sabbath, so writing is forbidden. Not much else allowed either, other than trudging off to the synagogue and having the law wailed at you. We really do need more colour in our religion.

Too sick to write, anyway.

~ Sunday 28 March ~

Still sick. Perhaps it's the sickness that comes of deep and dire dread of all that the future holds. I keep thinking of the virginal Diana Spencer, and what the moment must have felt like, when Charles slipped the engagement ring on her finger, sealing her fate: 'With this ring thy privacy is dead . . .' Did a door open for that instant, and let the chill future in? Did she have a fleeting glimpse of what lay ahead of her, the relentless media scrutiny, the public spotlight piercing her every action, analysing her every frown. And for that moment, as her eternity froze, did she shiver, both thrilled and mortified by the sheer terror of it all?

Because the angst she may or may not have gone through is just a gnat compared to the camel-load of troubles in store for me. You see, I'm going to give birth to the Son of God, his final Word, his incarnate Self, Emmanuel, etc., etc. Go away and read the New Testament if you want all the titles. Almost as many as the cast list in an Andrew Lloyd Webber musical.

According to Yahweh (only God could have such a weird name, and we Jews aren't slow at coming forward where weird names are concerned), I'm carrying humanity's ultimate hope. Just think what a job description like that does to a fourteen-year-old girl. The dark wounds ahead, which will break my heart. Having to put up with the incomprehensible ways of my friend, Yahweh – flip through the Old Testament and see the dark moods he's prone to. Having people project onto me the attributes of the momma they never had.

Time fails me to tell of having a Beatles' song written in your honour. Or having to do guest appearances at dumps like Lourdes and Walsingham. On my sojourns to chilly

4

Norfolk I feel like wearing an overcoat, with the winds whipping straight off the Urals – hardly the place to be clad in skimpy Palestinian national costume.

And then all those slinky statues, purveyed by ecclesiastical boutiques: they really make me weep. I look as if I'd burst a gut giving birth to anyone's child, let alone the Son of God.

What takes the biscuit, or rather regurgitates the biscuit, is the thought of having to put up with the millions, who for century after century will bleat after me with the pettiest of petitions:

'Mother Mary, don't let me be sea-sick when I cross the Channel.'

'Mother Mary, let me find a parking space.'

'Mother Mary, help me pass my Domestic Science GCSE.' (What have the complexities of the National Curriculum to do with me, I ask you?)

Not to mention the requests that tug at the heartstrings:

'Mother Mary, don't let me be pregnant yet again.'

'Mother Mary, keep him safe on the Somme.'

'Mother Mary, don't let her die of TB.'

'Hail Mary, full of grace' rings in my ears every second, morning, noon and night, like tinnitus with a Theology degree. 'Hail Mary, full of wind' would be a more appropriate epitaph, given that we Jews curiously use the same word 'wind' both for God's Spirit and a gale. 'I maketh my bed in my sickness,' as the psalm goes.

~ Monday 29 March ~

Sorry about yesterday. I felt so very ill. More myself today. You'll be wondering who the hell I am, what on earth I was going on about. Let me start by introducing myself. My name's Miriam in Hebrew, Maria in Greek and Latin, Mary in English. My parents, Joachim and Anna, run the local pizza restaurant here in Nazareth, a popular eating place for the Roman soldiers who occupy these parts – and every other part of the world if it comes to that.

Not hiding my light under a bushel (I hazard my son will make that phrase famous in about thirty years' time), for a fourteen-year-old, I'm a bright girl. I'm fluent in four languages, Hebrew, Greek, Latin and English, which is quite an achievement when the latter hasn't even been invented yet. I sometimes wonder whether those ancient Brits will ever learn to communicate. Daubing themselves in woad and grunting at the Romans seems about their limit.

Mathematically, I'm quite advanced for my age, two thousand years advanced to be precise. I'll have to wait sixteen hundred years before I can talk about calculus with Isaac Newton, nineteen hundred years before I can explain to Albert Einstein where he went wrong with his theory of relativity, and two thousand years before I can tip off Andrew Wiles how to solve Fermat's Last Theorem. If you think that's difficult, you just try to solve his first. Finding it alone took me seventeen centuries.

You won't be surprised to learn that I'm also an accomplished musician. Not for me the timbrels, with which the local maidens while away their time, fiercely beating them on their ample hips and buttocks – eat your heart out, Marquis de Sade! (Thinking about it, he probably would.) For me it's the harp. Grade VIII on the harp to be precise, the only musical instrument around in these times worth bothering with, just the thing to top off my hero King David's 278 psalms. (Yes, I do know only 150 made it into the Book of Common Prayer, but you should see the 128 which were expurgated. The banned Sixties' hit 'Je t'aime' is tame compared to David's hot stuff.)

~ *Tuesday 30 March* ~

If I'm such a clever girl, how did I end up pregnant? It's a long story. I know that I've always been different from the others, what with this strange relationship I have. Not with a man, but with time. Everyone else I know lives in the present; but my present seems to combine with the past and future to make a weird mosaic of eternity. One minute I'll be in the here and now, with the Zealot resistance drenching themselves as they sabotage the Romans' aqueducts – hot on courage, cool on intelligence, those Zealots. The next minute I'll be back a thousand years dancing with King David as he stormed Jerusalem, no underwear under his kilt like the true Scot he was. A minute later, I'll breeze forward a similar span and glimpse Crusader slogging it out with Moslem over who owns Palestine. Why all the competition over a land strife-torn since the day of creation defeats me. Very generous of Yahweh to promise it to us, when no one else in their right mind would touch it with a galley oar. Some promise that was!

You know, the future is a frightening place to sojourn, mostly dark terror-filled clouds of grief and heartbreak with just the occasional sunlight shaft of joy. I envy my fellow Jews, rooted in the present, even an oppressive present of Italian cooking, Italian driving and a paranoid Italian government.

So how did all this back to the future stuff end up with me being pregnant? As I said, it's a long story. Sufficient unto the day the time travel thereof. I hazard my son will say something like that too.

~ Wednesday 31 March ~

You see, all that time travel and dark forebodings had been much more intense of late, coming to a head last Thursday. At first, when I saw him, I thought the future had travelled into my room, rather than me surfing the future. Certainly he wasn't like the local boys or the local militia, no Jewish nose (or Roman nose if it comes to that), no swarthy features. But blond as blond can be, with a shimmering of light around his body as if the sun were behind him. I clicked when I saw the talaria (Now there's a word for an educated girl! Look it up in the Oxford English Dictionary rather than expect me to explain): This is an angel in your room, girl, or your name's not Miriam BarPizzaman.

Our rabbis are fiercely divided on the subject of angels. Some talk as if their guardian angel is beside them every moment, a spiritual cross between a personal organizer and a mobile phone. Others splutter that angels are a figment of an overheated religious imagination, and that they wouldn't be seen dead with them, a self-fulfilling prophecy if ever there was one. All this hiatus gave rise to a recent leader in the *Jerusalem Times*, '. . . not since the Exile has the Jewish Church risked such schism . . .' The *Jerusalem Times* is always coming up with leaders like that, since there's not a subject on God's earth that the rabbis aren't divided on. But schism never comes.

I was agnostic about angels until I went to Mons. I tended to hang around the Western Front a bit, intensely, passionately sorry for all the carnage, the pain, the heart-break. I really hurt for all those men on both sides being led like sheep to the slaughter. But Mons was different. True enough, the same blood-bath, the same mud, the same stench of rotting flesh, the same cries of agony. The difference was the lights, angelic lights hovering over the battlefield like Yahweh had hovered over the chaotic abyss on the first day of creation, somehow bringing comfort to screaming men beyond comfort. I know I go on about Yahweh and his inscrutable ways, but when it comes to the crunch, he's an absolute brick.

I lingered at Mons for a while, so long that I was late for tea at Nazareth. While I munched Momma's charred lamb and fig pizza, I thought a while and became a convinced angelophile (a word you won't find in the OED since I've just invented it, meaning *a friend of angels*).

~ Thursday 1 April ~

Played a brilliant April fool on Momma. I claimed an order had come in from the Jerusalem Rabbinical College for a 100 manna and quail pizzas. 'Where can a modern Jewish girl like me get hold of manna these days? Even if I could, the stuff wouldn't keep for the two days' donkey ride to Jerusalem. Do they think I'm Moses or something?' she wailed, the colour draining from her face.

Let me explain that when our great-great . . . great-great grandparents had escaped from Egypt and were feeling just a touch peckish in the wilderness, good old Yahweh sent them manna and quails to eat. Like all of Yahweh's gifts, there was a catch. He obviously twigged that some of my more mercenary ancestors might try to make a financial killing out of the manna futures' market. To thwart them he gave the stuff a short best-before-date, so short it had to be consumed on the day it appeared. Sure enough, some of my canny forebears tried to hoard the manna to force up the price. But the bottom dropped out of the market the next day when they found the stuff had gone sour overnight, consumed with worms. Hence Momma's worry about keeping her pizzas fresh in transit.

I decided to put her out of her misery. 'It's a joke, Momma,' I exclaimed, 'April fool?' I ducked as she threw the hot pizza pan at me. I'll have to break it to her soon. We can't have hot pizza pans injuring the Saviour of the World.

Which brings me back to my explanation as to why I'm heavy with child. Well, not that heavy as yet. Judging from that book about pregnancy I brought back from a daytrip to London recently, I should only be about one ounce heavier than I was last week. But given how sick I've been since last Thursday, I reckon I've lost more than half a stone. So 'light with child' would be nearer the mark.

Anyway, here in my room was this gorgeous angel. 'Hail, thou art highly favoured, the Lord is with thee: blessed art thou among women,' he intoned, in a sing-song voice. Why angels always address you in Elizabethan English, I cannot imagine, especially as nearly all the angels I have encountered suffer from a lisp. You'd think that being God's messengers, they'd try and get street-wise and develop some media cred.

As I furrowed my brow puzzling over all this, he mistook my bewilderment for awe.

'Fear not, Mary, for thou hast found favour with God. And behold, thou shalt conceive in thy womb . . .'

'At least that rules out an ectopic pregnancy,' I consoled myself.

'. . . And bring forth a son, and shalt call his name Jesus,' he continued. He didn't half say the name Jesus in a funny way, his vocal chords doing a shiver on the long 'e', his head slightly bowing. We've got lots of Jesuses around here, Jesus the butcher, Jesus the chippie, Jesus the farmhand. I've never heard the name said so hesitantly. Perhaps his lisp was giving him trouble.

But it didn't stop him going on. 'He shall be great and shall be called the son of the Highest . . .' He then began to rattle off all those titles I'd referred you to in my earlier diary entry.

'Hang on a minute,' I interrupted him. 'I got hold of this book on my last trip to London. You don't fall pregnant until you get up to a certain activity. And I haven't got up to it. So how can I be conceiving in my womb and all that jazz?'

'I wath coming to sthat,' he said huffily, his lisp deteriorating. 'The Holy Ghost shall come upon thee, and the power of the highest shall overshadow thee . . .'

'And what is that supposed to mean?' I demanded.

'Virgin birth, babe,' he explained, suddenly lapsing into cool-dude speak. 'Conception without sex, the antithesis of what the human race has been striving for since the dawn of time.'

'But that's impossible,' I countered. 'David Jenkins said it couldn't be done.'

'Well you're going to surprise him!' the angel responded.

'Like heck I am. If you think I'm going to have a kid at fourteen and throw away a brilliant academic career, you've got another think coming, sunshine boy!'

At least that's what I meant to say. What I actually said was, 'Behold the handmaid of the Lord. Be it unto me according to thy word.' That's the trouble with the Angelus

11

– it really does soak into your consciousness, and comes out at the most inappropriate times.

~ *Friday 2 April* ~

Not a Good Friday. Visions of the future, thirty-odd years on. A desperately dark day, weeping, betrayals, a horrible death for some mother's son. Sharp pains in my stomach draw me back to the present, with a little bleeding from you-know-where. Yahweh, as always, proves an ally with a sting in the tail.

'Don't worry, Mary, your problems are nothing compared to mine. I've been in pain, bleeding since the world began.'

~ *Sunday 4 April* ~

Feel so much better today, unbelievably, incredibly lighter, like eating wonderfully risen bread compared to that flat doughy stuff we Jews have to munch our way through at Passover time. I was up early, while it was yet dark, and just drank in the dawn. The sun glorious, its rays life-giving, every Spring thing bursting with the promise of life-to-come. Pregnant old me felt at one with the whole of creation, which certainly was a sea change to the dire, dark and gloomy night that had oppressed me these past few days.

On such a high that I share my secret with Momma and Poppa, complete with the positive pregnancy test confirmed by an angel. A big mistake. Taking his cue from Yahweh, Poppa goes into a sulk and Momma throws yet another pizza pan at me, wailing, 'How could a girl of mine, brought up as an orthodox Jewess, taught to cherish Moses and

Italian cooking, how could she behave in such a despicable, filthy way?'

I ducked as a further pizza pan hurtled through the air. 'Yes, my girl. You can learn to duck and dodge. Today pizza pans; tomorrow stones, you adulteress!'

~ Monday 5 April ~

By this morning, Poppa was more controlled, 'Miriam, don't worry, it's not your fault. Someone took advantage of you, didn't they? You were out in the wilderness where no one could hear your cries for help, weren't you? You don't have to invent all that angel nonsense. Just tell me which Roman soldier did this to you, and we'll get the Zealot boys to sort him out with their Circumcision Surprise.'

'But Poppa, no one laid a finger on me,' I protested. 'The Holy Spirit overshadowed me and now I'm with Yahweh's child.' Yahweh's Ultimate Child if half of what that angel said to me comes true.

Yet another pizza pan flew through the air, missing me and glancing off Poppa's shoulder, an unsubtle cue that Momma was about to make an entrance. 'With Yahweh's child? With Yahweh's child? That excuse is as old as creation itself, used by every trollop to try to pull one over on her cuckold. Yahweh indeed! It's man that gives you a child, not Yahweh. He just gives us a headache.' Now you'll realize where I get my cynical attitude to the Almighty from.

Momma wailed on and on. I had recently been watching the video of *Pride and Prejudice*: Momma was Mrs Bennet to a tee. Except that since Momma had only one daughter and not five to get off her hands, I couldn't see what all the fuss was about. But that didn't stop her going on, and on. 'You would go and do this, just when I'd got you matched

13

with so respectable a personage as Joe the Chip, so gentle, so good, so religious, so wealthy...'

She drawled the first syllable so that it came out weeeealthy, at the same time a misty look came into her eyes. 'So wealthy with all those replacement windows he's been fitting recently. He won't look twice at you now. He can afford to be choosy. He doesn't have to take damaged goods. You'll have to go round, do the honourable thing and let him in on your little act. He'll call the whole thing off, I know it. And it'll break your Jewish momma's heart. It'll be the death of me.'

Betraying no signs of her immanent demise, she raged on and on, a succession of flying pizza pans punctuating each paragraph. As it says in Solomon's Book of Proverbs, 'Shun a Pizza Palace when there's wrath in the air.' I took off for a walk around the lake.

A storm whipped up the waters, mirroring Momma's ire. Yahweh obviously felt he owed me an explanation, 'Don't worry, Mary, peace is begotten in violence.' What is that supposed to mean, I ask you? When you're being showered with pizza pans, philosophy ain't much use. I'm sure that's one of Solomon's proverbs too.

~ Tuesday 6 April ~

The hardest journey in the world: A young girl wending her way to her fiancé to tell him that the child she is carrying in her womb isn't his. I steeled myself for an arsenal of chisels, coping saws, sliding bevels, marking gauges, carpenter's black edged pencils and sundry planks to be hurled my way. At least it would make a change from pizza pans.

Even so, my bowels turned to water the nearer I got to Joe's threshold. I hadn't even got a sniff of what opening gambit I could employ. For a start, pregnancy makes most women's brains feel foggy. On top of that, mine was a pretty big subject to introduce, the biggest in the history of the world, past, present and future. And since it hadn't happened before and wasn't going to happen again, there was no way I could surf the past and future to find a precedent from which I could take my cue. There were some rather curious goings-on in very Ancient Greece, when the gods took a half-day off from Mount Olympus and sported with local maidens. Nine months later a cluster of demi-god babies arrived – a memorable calling card if ever there was one. But entertaining though the legend was, I couldn't get an angle on it to introduce my own predicament. I haven't sported with anyone. We Jews have no Mount Olympus. And we only have one God, Yahweh, who definitely isn't into the sort of sensuous things that the Greek gods got up to. When Yahweh came down from the mountain, his calling card was the law, the Torah, carved on tablets of lifeless stone.

'Joe, what a wonderful dove-tail joint you've carved; you are so talented. Oh, by the way, I'm pregnant.' No chance. Just imagine the field day Freud and his ilk would have, associating dove-tail joints and impregnation.

'Joe, you're highly respected, a true son of Nazareth. Talking about sons, I'm going to give birth to the Son of God.' Too slick.

'Joe, there was this angel, honestly, I'm not making it up, and he told me I was with child, a special child with no human father.' That'd never work: Joe's a practical chap, with his feet on the ground, not given to wild religious speculation. You see my dilemma.

15

I needn't have worried. As soon as I entered his workshop, Joe, downing his retractable-blade trimming knife (Keep off, Freud!), ran over to me and embraced me so fondly, so warmly. 'Oh Mary, I'm so glad you've come,' he blurted out, staccato fashion. 'I'm so, so very pleased for you. I'll look after you. I'll protect you. Such an honour to be married to the Theotokos.'

'Theotowhat?' I asked, incredulous, thinking it was some new woodwork gadget that had addled his brain.

'Theotokos,' he corrected, 'It's Greek for God-bearer. What with his lisp, the angel had a bit of trouble getting his tongue around it, but then he explained it all in careful detail. *Theos*, second declension masculine meaning *God*, synthesized with *tokos*, second declension masculine meaning *bearer*. A wonderful word.'

'But I'm feminine,' I objected.

'Now, now, Mary, don't get into all that inclusive language debate. Let's leave that to the Americans. I'm just so thrilled. The angel explained it all to me. We've so much to look forward to. We'll never want for fish and bread again. And all my problems with tricky dove-tail joints will be over for ever and ever.'

On an exhilaration-high, he immediately started crooning Psalm 148, 'Praith him all histh angelths . . .' No prizes for guessing who taught him to sing like that.

Ah well, though I could do without the religious ecstasy, it's good to have someone on my side at last. It seems that peace was begotten in violence after all. That Yahweh's a wily old bird. That's the thing I'm learning about God – he's always right. Even so, I hope he'll change his mind and let me be called *Theotoke* – *toke* first declension feminine, as every Greek scholar knows. It's bad enough staging a virgin birth; pretending that virgin's a male really beggars belief.

~ Tuesday 27 April ~

Not much to write about these past three weeks. A resume: I'm still sick; Momma's still screaming; Poppa's still moody; Joe's still kind; Yahweh's still Yahweh. He's a funny sort of God. At times I sense he is carrying me, and I feel warm and protected. At other times he says something cutting and I feel so small. More often than not, when I really need him, he seems a million miles away. Then, like Gandalf in *Lord of the Rings*, he breezes in too huffy and too late, with never an apology.

I've been quite taken with *Lord of the Rings* recently. All that weird symbolism, the betrayals, the redemptions, the cosmic battle between good and evil, it sends shivers down my spine. 'Thank you for Tolkien,' I prayed one night, 'I enjoy seasoning reality with a little escapist fantasy.'

'Enjoy it while you can,' Yahweh quipped. 'Soon escapist fantasy will be your reality!' I'm thinking of taking an Open University Philosophy module, just so I can keep up with Yahweh's metaphysical bent. Otherwise, what's the use of a God who's an enigma?

~ Wednesday 28 April ~

I've certainly got something to write about today. Momma, riled by complaints about her mis-shapen pizzas, let the cat out of the bag. 'Just look at these pans,' she raged, waving them at her whining customers, 'What shape do you expect the pizzas to be with battered pans like these?'

Mistaking their stunned silence for interest, she continued, 'Let me tell you why they're battered. I've been using them to knock some sense into my good-for-nothing daughter. How we are going to be able to afford to feed another

17

mouth, when we can't even afford new pans, Yahweh knows! I've no need to tell you how this wretched Roman government has a down on single mothers and won't grant them a drachma in aid.'

Word soon got around after that. Those boys of my own age and young men in their twenties were the worst. They soon started leering at me, jeering, throwing stones, yelling 'adulteress'. They said other things as well, but I wouldn't want to shock you in a religious publication. Their hypocrisy sickens me, or would do if I wasn't sick already. Front seat in the synagogue on the Sabbath, all goodie-goodie and law-abiding. But once the Sabbath was over, lurking in the shady alleys of Nazareth, taking any girl who'd have them. Not that a girl gets much choice when these hyenas start prowling around. They're only mad at me because they think they missed out on the action.

~ Thursday 29 April ~

Things became even rougher today. The local louts got their act together and hustled me as I was drawing water from the well, pushing me around, tearing my clothes, 'Little Miriam's too good for the likes of us. She likes to play with Roman soldiers instead. Let's show her what we do with traitors!'

One of them yanked at my hair and dragged me through the streets, or rather through the street since Nazareth only has one, all the way to Joe's house, throwing me down on his step as they battered on the door.

'Good master,' they sneered, as Joe gazed somewhat bewilderedly at the crowd, with me at their feet. 'Good master, from her own mother's mouth, this woman stands condemned as an adulteress. In the law, Moses has laid down that such women should be stoned to death. You're her

18

betrothed, Joe, you're the one whose honour has been most insulted by her action. Here's a rock. You kick us off.'

Poor Joe: a skilled carpenter, a man of action, not a man of words. I could see he was out of his depth. I braced myself. So, Yahweh, so this is your great plan for the redemption of the world, is it, ending with my being battered before it even began?

'Let the one amongst you who is without sin, let him cast the first stone,' Joe pronounced, staring them all out. And with that he lifted me up, let me into the house and closed the door on them. Not that they caused any further trouble. They went away, the eldest first, their heads bowed with shame.

I flung my bruised arms around Joe and gave him a hug of deep gratitude. 'You were brilliant,' I enthused, 'So wise!'

'Oh, the words weren't mine,' Joe shrugged. I should have spotted the slight lisp. Now I know who the real author of his fine, succinct speech was. Good old Yahweh, sending his angel to the rescue. Last-Minute-Gandalf rides again! Perhaps, if I may venture a tiny criticism of the immortal, invisible God only wise, just a wee bit last minute for my liking, when I was the one in danger of getting my head smashed in.

~ Friday 30 April ~

Maybe I can understand why the local louts are as they are, with all this angst around about the dawn of a new aeon. We have been counting the years backwards for so long, that we're fast approaching the year nought, when we'll have to get used to the new-fangled habit of counting the years forward. We Jews have always written backwards and counted backwards, so where's the logic, I ask you, in counting

19

forwards? All the abacuses have had to be adapted in anticipation of the dreaded change-over date, a difficult operation (or at least difficult for my blockhead countrymen) involving turning them through 180 degrees.

And then there's the pension nightmare. Take my old dad – born in the year 35. If he achieves his biblical three score years and ten, then he'll die in the year 35 too under the new system. On paper, it'll look like an infant death. But in reality this 'infant' will have left a wife, daughter, and grandson (albeit a grandson-of-God). Try getting Social Security to work all that out!

On top of that, we have to put up with all the religious nuts. The most extreme fully expect the world to grind to a dead halt in the year nought, so have anticipated things somewhat and have taken themselves off to the Dead Sea, a dead halt if ever there was one. They whittle away their time there writing scrolls predicting dire gloom. Too embarrassed by all the colourful language that has flowed out of their stylus, for very shame they then have to hide their work in caves. I suppose that's their equivalent of the top shelf in Borders. All this frantic activity keeps them occupied, though. And, more importantly, keeps them out of our hair.

The high priests, never ones to be over fettered by religion's demands, want us to light a candle on New Aeon's Eve, chanting, 'Yahweh, I've been going backwards long enough. Now lead me forwards! menA.' Shows how little they know of Yahweh. As far as my experience goes, he always seems to lead you in circles.

Anyway, you can see why there's all this angst around. When the time comes (or goes) I'm hoping to crawl into a cave or barn somewhere, and miss the whole charade.

~ Saturday 1 May ~

A bit of a problem, Labour Day coinciding with the Sabbath, celebrating work by not doing any at all. I suppose it has the perverse logic of Yahweh about it.

~ Sunday 2 May ~

'Miriam, take to the hills!' A funny way to be greeted by one's fiancé, but it seems his friend the lisping angel has had another word in his ear. It would be better, apparently, if I steered clear of Nazareth for a few months, out of harm's and Momma's pizza pans' way. The cunning plan is to shunt me off to Auntie Liz and Uncle Zech Cohen's farm, high on the Judean moors. Certainly my rounding figure won't shock the local inhabitants, since apart from Zech and Liz the place is populated solely by sheep and goats, and very broad-minded sheep and goats at that.

~ Monday 3 May ~

7 am: Depart from Nazareth on Joe's ass, with my intended walking beside me. Momma wakes even the dead with her wailing litany, mourning the loss of her dear daughter, 'How will I ever get by without my little darling, my sweet innocent child,' she moans. The pizzas will be in better shape for a start.

Her cries arouse the local louts. Bleary-eyed, they give me a sending off party by showering me with pebbles. Still half-asleep, their aim is none too good. In fact it is appalling – these schmucks wouldn't hit a Goliath at ten paces. Which is fortunate for me and for Yahweh's incarnation, not to mention Joe and his ass. Even then I get a glancing blow on

21

the forehead which leaves a nasty gash. The pebble's hurler must have been aiming at something else, and struck lucky. Or perhaps it was thrown by Yahweh to remind me that from pain there is no escaping.

~ Tuesday 4 May ~

5 pm: Arrive at Lone Moors Farm, Judea. Uncle Zech is obviously in one of his moods (he's a priest, so he takes after Yahweh), because he greets me without a single word. Joe carries my bags to the guestroom above the barn and then sets off on his way, abandoning me to this wild and bleak place. A Cold Comfort Farm if ever there was one – a taciturn old man and a thousand bleating sheep.

The whole place defrosted when Auntie Liz breezed in, ruddy faced from her climb to feed the lambs cosseted in the hill-top barn. Despite the gruelling exercise which is the lot of every hill-farmer's wife, she was obviously putting on weight by the stone. 'Ee, Miriam, it's good to see thee. I'm reeght favoured, that t' mother of my Lord should come to me.'

Her broad twang had a slight lisp, giving away that my good friend the angel had gossiped news of my pregnancy far beyond Nazareth. 'That bloody angel, can't he keep his celestial lip zipped!' At least that was what I meant to say. Instead I found myself trilling the Magnificat, the first canticle in the Book of Common Prayer, Evensong, 1662 years early. Auntie Liz bopped to the beat, Uncle Zech looked as sullen and as obdurate as ever, a right party-pooper if ever there was one.

'Ee, Miriam, when I saw thee standing there, in t' bloom o' motherhood, my own bairn leapt in my womb! Blessed be Yahweh, giving us both the gift of children!'

I stared at Auntie Liz, open-mouthed. She was well past the age for being a grandmother, let alone a mother. Miraculous births are breaking out like wildfire. It's getting like John Wyndham's *The Midwich Cuckoos*. You know, the science fiction classic where every woman in Midwich conceives after a mysterious alien visitation . . . Not that I'm a big fan of sci-fi. Honestly, the incredible stuff they expect you to swallow!

~ Wednesday 5 May ~

It's so quiet up here. I couldn't get off to sleep because of the pregnant silence (you can say that again!) and then, just as I was nodding off, a dawn chorus of bleating sheep interrupted my troubled dreams. Uncle Zech clearly had had a bad night too, brooding over a breakfast of honey and wild locust berries with a stony silence. The price of lamb is at an all-time low, perhaps that's what's worrying him.

I raised the subject as we womenfolk washed the dishes. 'No, lass, we're doing fine,' Auntie Liz assured me. By the way, forgive me if I don't continue recording Auntie Liz's dialect verbatim. Otherwise this diary will start looking like another James Herriot epic.

'Zech's diversified and has a good market for his lambs down at the temple,' Auntie Liz explained. 'Come Passovertime, they can't get enough sheep down there, all that sacrificing and reminiscing that goes on. We just count ourselves lucky that it was lamb's blood and not crocodile blood that our ancestors daubed on their Egyptian doorposts. A crocodile farm would never come off up here.'

We Jews are always remembering that dark night. How the angel of death, curiously vegetarian, by-passed lamb-smeared Jewish homes and struck the Egyptian first-born

23

instead, who, understandably, hadn't had the foresight to decorate their exteriors with a fresh coat of lamb's blood. It was the very best of times for us Jews, akin to England winning the World Cup in 1966. It was the very worst of times for Egyptians and lambs. That's the trouble with magnificent acts of redemption: there's always someone who loses out.

~ Thursday 6 May ~

'So what is troubling Uncle Zech, then?' I broached the subject once again, as Auntie Liz and I washed the breakfast dishes.

'Oh, it's a bit delicate, really,' she began, blushing a deep crimson. 'Yahweh decreed that my barren old age should be punctuated with a special baby. The exertion of it all,' she looked away in embarrassment, her crimson turning even deeper, 'The exertion of all this late-flowering lust must have given your uncle a slight stroke. He's been speechless ever since.' Despite her awkwardness, she gave me a little smile. We were girls together, after all.

~ Friday 7 May ~

Uncle Zech toddles off to the temple, with a few sheep wagging their unsuspecting tails behind him. I chat with Auntie Liz, over the dishes yet again – it feels as if we're rooted to the kitchen sink. 'How does Uncle get through all those long services without saying a word?'

'Well, they're not that long when he's the celebrant. Just a few inarticulate moans and a brief silence, and he's through. His new style is very popular; t' other priests are green with envy over t' big congregations he draws.'

~ Sunday 9 May ~

'Dr Luke'll be calling round for my regular check-up today,' Auntie Liz informed me. 'It might be a good idea if he gives you a look over too. That nasty gash on your head seems to be taking a long time to heal.'

Dr Luke, it appears, is a foreigner. Though the Zealot National Front have a big campaign about boycotting Gentile doctors in the Israeli National Health Service, I suppose a girl in my condition can't afford to be choosy. I realize our Jewish doctors wouldn't taint their hands touching a girl with the whiff of adultery about her. I can't say I blame them. We Jews are so obsessed with purity and impurity: Were a Jewish doctor to treat dubious old me, then immediately there'd be 99 righteous persons who he'd lose from his practice.

It seems that Auntie Liz is in a similar predicament to me, with the local practice washing their hands of her. They wouldn't believe anyone of her age could be expecting, so they wrote the whole thing off as a phantom pregnancy, then obesity, then a growth, despite her insistence that she was with child. Her persistence got her struck off their list.

Meanwhile, Dr Luke, a foreigner in a land where xeno-phobia is king, was at his wit's end, wandering around Palestine with his little black bag, people spitting at him, yelling 'Gentile dog' rather than availing themselves of his healing skills. He was only too pleased to take on Auntie Liz. Both needed each other to be their last resort.

~ Monday 10 May ~

Dr Luke didn't call round until late last night, rushed off his feet with calls. It seems that the doctor who formerly had no patients is now a victim of his own success. Or rather Auntie Liz's success, since she has acted as sort of practice manager for him, building up quite a clientele for him, gleefully conscripting patients deemed impure under the strict Jewish law. Her fellow shepherds, for instance, commit the heinous sin of watching their flocks rather than resting on the Sabbath, so are no-go zones where orthodox Jewish doctors are concerned. Dr Luke has made a real hit, prescribing Benylin to cure their bronchitis (an inevitable consequence of all those nights out on the cold, damp Judean hills).

He is a real dish. He examined me so tenderly, clearly a superb doctor. Although he does have some weird equipment. For instance, he gave me what he termed an ultrasound scan. I won't go into the gruesome details, but the long and short of it was that he rubbed some honey on my tummy (groovy!) and then drew an instant picture of my baby on a glass screen. Concern furrowed his brow. 'I'm a bit worried about the ring above his head,' he commented, curtly.

He looked so troubled, I decided to let him into my secret, and explained that the ring was probably a halo. He didn't seem in the least bit surprised. 'I've got an insight into the eternal too, you know. Where do you think I got the idea for the scanner from?' he said, smiling shrewdly.

~ Wednesday 12 May ~

A bit bored. Nothing much happens up here, apart from lamb for breakfast, dinner, tea and supper. I can taste the stuff in my dreams. I just hope that all this mutton doesn't have an untoward effect on my unborn babe. I would hate my son to grow up with a lamb fixation.

Auntie Liz promises me that tomorrow she's staging something that will break the tedium.

~ Thursday 13 May ~

Auntie Liz up well before dawn, baking countless dainties: lamb vol au vents, lamb crisps, lamb nuggets, lamb sausages on sticks, lamb rolls, lamb surprise (the surprise is it's just lamb), lamb tart . . . The reason for all this industry is that it's Auntie's turn to host the BMU – the Barren Mothers' Union, an exclusive group of women from the scriptures who gave birth in their barren old age to a special son of God. Like me, they've all homed in on the eternal and can move through the ages.

They were clearly not too chuffed about my being present, in that technically I'm not entitled to membership, since I'm a virgin mother and not a barren one. Auntie loyally stuck up for me, as did Hannah, sweet, calm and beautiful Barren Mother of Samuel the prophet. Mrs Manoah (the Book of Judges doesn't give her a first name), Barren Mother of Samson, lion-tamer, womanizer and temple-demolisher, gave me a sour look. 'If we start letting virgins in, who knows where it'll end. You're either barren or you're out, that's what I say.'

Shy, handsome Rachel, Barren Mother of Benjamin, Joseph and his Amazing Technicolour Dreamcoat, stuck up for me. 'Where else can the poor girl go? The Virgin Mothers' Union folded centuries ago, due to members failing to stay the course. Let's make her an associate member.'

All the other Barren Mothers agreed, bar one, so I was duly enrolled. Whoopee!

The Barren Mothers' Union are back again to replenish their ample tanks with Auntie's lamb dainties. Given the fuss they made last time over my being there, I did wonder why Bathsheba (King David's fecund mistress, not noted for her barrenness) was a member until Hannah explained in a hushed whisper, 'She holds the copyright to her husband David's psalms. We're only allowed to sing them on the condition she attends.'

I've mentioned David before, the Cliff Richard of ancient Palestine, writing lyric after lyric which trips off the tongue. His *Og, the King of Basan* topped the charts for a record sixteen months.

The meeting proceeded with a regular feature, Psalm 168, a wailing litany against barrenness (pointed according to the Parish Psalter):

> It's terrible/to be/barren: no result to show for night af/ter night/of/sex. No child's cry/piercing the/darkness: no babe hang/ing at/your/breasts.

'And the disadvantages?' I wanted to ask. Then I remembered that I was without sin, so thought better of it.

Eventually this litany switched to Psalm 207, a tirade against conceiving in one's old age:

> Having to/get back in/to sex: when you thought it was all/safely be/hind/you.

('You just wait for Viagra, girls!' saucy Sarah interjected.)

> Having a child's cry/pierce your/slumbers: a babe gnawing your/wiz/ened/breasts.

Some people are never satisfied.

~ Monday 24 May ~

Auntie Liz and I trudge with our dirty linen to the local stream, a tributary of the infamous River Jordan which bisects our land like a vein running a leaf's length. Auntie is very heavy with child, so by the time we reach the stream she is all but exhausted by the walk and her heavy load of Uncle's smalls. I take over, plunging the washing repeatedly under the gurgling stream's surface, scrubbing hard-to-shift stains against the abrasive rocks on the water's edge. Auntie sits, shaking her head as she watches me, 'Ee, Miriam, I ought to be doing this for you, not you for me. The mother of my Lord shouldn't be caught up with such menial tasks. I feel so ashamed.'

'Don't worry, Auntie,' I reassured her, 'Let it be so for now. If the mother of your Lord didn't do the washing, then we'd all be stuck with dirty underwear.' Never mind Solomon – I think I'll start recording my own book of proverbs.

~ Thursday 27 May ~

Auntie hosts the BMU for a third and final guzzle. Mrs Manoah is full of herself. She's just been on a time trip to an America in the throws of feminism and on a rainy evening had completed a PhD in Women's Studies. 'Female persons, don't you think it's a disgrace that whenever Yahweh gives a barren woman a baby, it always turns out to be a son? It's about time he magicked up a daughter, if he's as fair as he makes out.'

'Yahweh, fair??!' I thought to myself.

Mrs Manoah's bandwagon was taken up by Sarah (wife, sister? of Abraham, Barren Mother of Isaac), who asked whether, since we now admitted virgins, shouldn't we also admit nuns?

'No nuns,' Bathsheba snapped. 'They'd force us to sing my David's songs to plainsong. He always wanted jazz with harp accompaniment, and that's what we'll stick to.'

After a fierce debate a compromise was agreed. Mother Teresa's mother would henceforth be admitted to meetings, as a token mother both of a nun and a girl. Not a lot of people know that Mother Teresa's mother was called Gertrude the Sax, a famous jazz singer. They do now.

~ Monday 7 June ~

Dr Luke makes an early morning call. 'You look a bit peaky, Miriam,' he confides. 'I think you need a break from all this.' Too right! The solitude of this forlorn and far away place, coupled with lamb, morning, noon and night and topped off by weekly visitations from exceedingly old women are all getting me down.

Luke and I whisk off through two thousand years of time and pop up in the hustle and bustle of central London. The traffic, the smell, the noise, the rubbish: certainly a contrast from Liz and Zech's hills. After an hour, it gets too much for us. Even a Judea pebble-dashed with sheep droppings seems attractive compared to all this high angst. Heartened by a sign, 'Aiming to restore the calm . . .', we steel into Westminster Abbey, to get our breaths back.

Some hope! There's a clergyman having a furious row with an organist, both bawling at the other, while another organist blares out an impromptu performance, a nasty little ditty that clearly Stockhausen composed while nursing a migraine. We get no further than the entrance till, since we're not carrying the right currency, apparently. Dollars,

Deutschmarks, Euros, even Sterling are all welcome. Drachmas and mites sadly not, so we are excluded. 'My temple should be a house of prayer,' my old friend Yahweh whispers in my ear. Sometimes I feel so very sorry for him. Our antics must break his incomprehensible heart.

Obviously we haven't quite mastered the basics of time travel, in that instead of returning to Judea, we miss the place by over fifty miles and end up in some remote spot called Gadarene on the shores of Lake Galilee. Still, all is not lost since the place boasts the best, if illegal, pork take-away in the Promised Land. We queue for ages. Clearly, I'm not the only Jew to be sick of lamb, with so many of my fellow countrymen risking breaking the Torah to give their tired kosher taste-buds a change.

Luke buys me a Mega Hot Dog (drachmas and mites acceptable here), which I intend to eat as we stroll around the lake. When it comes to it, the sight of the stuff turns my stomach. I hurl the bap over the cliffs in disgust, hot dog, or rather hot pig, tumbling into the sea. I'm obviously stuck with lamb.

~ *Monday 14 June* ~

Luke and I decide to give London another go. Steering clear of churches, we wander into a religious bookshop, with Luke letting out squeals of delight as he pours over the Mariolatry section. 'Look at this, Miriam, just read what this bloke's saying about you. He claims Uncle Zech is the father of your unborn child.'

I can see that this would give a bit more oomph to the rather tedious festival of my Visitation to Auntie Elizabeth's (Book of Common Prayer: 2 July). But I ask you, Uncle Zech?! Dr Luke had to prescribe a double dose of Viagra to

31

enable him to get up to what he got up to with Auntie Liz, let alone anyone else. And even then, the exertion made him speechless. Uncle Zech, in your dreams!

A paperback, *A Conspiracy of Silence*, poses the hoary chestnut that if my virgin pregnancy was the most miraculous in the history of creation, how come I kept so quiet about it? Especially when I could have played it like a trump card to get me and my son out of many a tricky situation. For instance, whenever people doubt him, or round on him, all I have to do is to draw their attention to miraculous origins to remind them of his divine credentials. A ruse that should floor even Jeremy Paxman.

The first flaw in this theory is that it forgets how prone we Jews are to amnesia. It's a curious thing, considering how much we go on about remembering, how much more we actually forget. We forget the terrible revenge Yahweh wreaks on those who disobey him, and wander off, whoring after other gods, as if we hadn't got a care in the world. We forget the kindness of Yahweh, delivering us from not one but two mass exiles, and throw that tender care back in his face. And our scriptures are peppered with people forgetting. Take my favourite epic about my hero, David. One day the boy David is anointed king in the presence of his brothers, the next day those same brothers deride him for even thinking of taking on Goliath, surely a king's job if ever there was one. And so it goes on. We Jews have short memories: 'Of the works of Yahweh there is much forgetting', as Solomon's proverb puts it. Even a virgin birth is only a nine-day wonder here.

Another flaw in this theory is its lack of imagination. I remember how tongue-tied and embarrassed Momma was when she spluttered out the Facts of Life, and how I blushed deep crimson when I heard them. I'm struck as

32

dumb as Uncle Zech when gynaecological peculiarities are on the agenda. Just picture the scene, thirty years on:

Cue boat reeling on a choppy Lake Galilee. Enter me from the hold, addressing the eight burly fishermen struggling against the storm:

'Excuse me interrupting, boys, but you know this Jesus you're following?'

'Yeah?'
'Well, I didn't become pregnant with him in the usual way!'
'Oh really? And which usual way is that, then?'

Cue seedy male laughter.

Cue A Conspiracy of Silence *being binned.*

Luke reads out loud from another book, which has me being raped by a Roman soldier. The piece of prose is a wee bit too lurid for the normally sanctified air of a religious bookshop, and several punters shuffle out, their disgust undisguised. These English are so uptight.

Liaison à la Rome was obviously a possibility that dawned on the local blockheads in Nazareth who hurled stones at me. The author of this book, however, writes as if he was the first brain for two millennia to catch on to the idea.

The weak points in his brilliant theory are:

1. It didn't happen. I for one should know. It's less than three months on and even a very repressed memory would give a bit of an inkling as to what went on.
2. Most of the Roman soldiers around our way are gay. Their membership of the Lesbian and Gay Legions

33

Movement guaranteed them a one-way ticket to the backwater of the Empire. Where do you think the term *camp* came from, if not from the lays of glorious Rome? How the Roman Empire survived more than a generation defeats me.

3. In all the thousands, if not millions, of paintings of my son, have you seen just one depicting him with a Roman nose?

Luke found yet another book which wondered whether my unborn child was a clone. I fell out of the shop laughing at that one. Mind you, Momma had thought of calling me Dolly rather than Miriam . . .

~ Part Two ~

~ Wednesday 23 June ~

The day has arrived. Auntie writhing, and groaning and shrieking, 'Oi, oi, oi,' a sine qua non of birth in the Middle East. Uncle pacing the floor in silent anguish. Me, boiling up pan after pan of water – Dr Luke is a tea addict and requires six cups an hour when he's hard at work. And the work is hard: Hour after hour Auntie strains, muscles atrophied for thirty years suddenly being called on to do their stuff. Just after dusk the waters break, gallon upon gallon, like Noah's flood. 'A right little water baby this one will be,' quips Luke, looking prophetic.

~ Thursday 24 June ~

Virtually on the stroke of midnight the child is born, a great cue for a song by Johnny Mathis. Auntie Liz had opted for birth to be as natural as possible, on straw on the barn floor, where she had eased so many lambs into the world.

Auntie spelled out the real reason for her choice: 'Uncle Zech would have gone wild if we'd let all the blood and gore contaminate the house. He'd have to ritually cleanse himself for months afterwards before the temple would re-issue his priest's licence.' The prospect of the sombre and silent Uncle Zech breaking his respectability and going wild seemed intriguingly attractive, coupled with the unworthy thought (certainly unworthy for the Virgin Mary) that if Uncle hadn't gone wild nine months before, he'd have saved himself all this worry over his precious priestly purity.

As the baby boy slithered into the world, the watching

sheep in their pens started to sink to their knees, like characters in some Thomas Hardy poem. I shooed them upright,
'Not yet, you dolts, you're six months too early!' Even so, I
could see why they were moved. The wonder of new life: A
tiny baby, bright red, swaddled in a coat of camel's hair
which Luke had found lying around, drinking from a breast
which Auntie had thought would have remained dry for
ever. Troubled by a silence which seemed eerie after the
incessant crying which had filled the night, Uncle Zech
stumbled through the gloomy farmyard to see whether
elderly mother and new-born child had survived; fervently
hoping it might be so, as Thomas Hardy would have said
– at least, would have said once I'd whispered the words
into his ear.

~ Friday 25 June ~

The book on pregnancy I brought back from our day trip
to London (although what a religious bookshop was doing
selling such a book, I shudder to think) counsels that the
day after a glorious birth is a bit of an anti-climax – a
veritable Boxing Day of cold turkey and stale trimmings.

You can say that again! Uncle Zech's relatives visited en
masse, the Addams Family to a tee, but without the finesse
and elegance. They snatched the day-old infant off Auntie,
passing him from each to each like a line-up, frantic for a
try at Twickenham. 'What you going to register him as,
then?' they whispered to Auntie, when they'd got tired of
their game of pass the baby. 'It'll have to be Zechariah, after
his father.'

'If Zechariah was up to fathering him,' I heard another
gorgon say, not so *sote voce*. I caught an amused twinkle in
Luke's eye.

'He will be called John, of Yahweh,' Auntie pronounced in stentorian tones which sadly did nothing to abate the rudeness of her relatives-in-law.

'John, John, what on earth do you want to call him John for? We've no one called John in our family.' The word 'our' was emphasized to make it clear that Auntie Liz, Dr Luke and I were definitely intruders.

'Ah, she's got the baby-blues, she's off her head. Take no notice of her. Let's go and find Zechariah. He'll soon put his foot down.'

I followed them out of the bedroom to the kitchen, where Uncle Zech was sitting at the table, scratching with a stylus onto a wax plate, painstakingly copying the scriptures. If you've ever tried to write Hebrew, you'll know what I mean by painstakingly.

Without a by or leave, the eldest of his relatives snatched the plate off him, and scratched on it, 'What do you want to call your child?'

With a rare display of fury, Uncle snatched the spoiled plate back, writing, 'I may be dumb, but I'm not deaf, you idiot. Talk to me!'

'What are you calling your son?' they shouted.

Uncle slowly wrote the words, 'He shall be called JOHN!' And then he wrote something else, which, as one spotless and without sin, I find myself unable to repeat. But it had the desired effect.

'Well, if that's your attitude, we'll take ourselves off. We only came to help. Of all the daftest things, having a child out here in the sticks at an age when you and that trollop you married should have known better. We know when we're not wanted.' And with that they departed, grumbling all the way. When Yahweh bids us to love our enemies, he is good enough to give us relatives to practise on.

Not that Uncle took any notice of them. He was singing – yes, his voice had returned. And not just any old song, but the Benedictus (that star of the Book of Common Prayer's Matins) in a beautiful tenor voice that belied his old age. Eat your heart out, Pavarotti!

~ Saturday 26 June ~

I lie abed overhearing Uncle and Auntie having a furious row. No one can doubt that Uncle's powers of speech are fully recovered. 'Look, woman, it's the Sabbath and the Torah says you do no work on the Sabbath, so you're not to change him.'

'Sabbath or no Sabbath, I haven't waited sixty years for a child to leave him wallowing in his filth. The poor little thing not only stinks, he's wet through, absolutely saturated. He'll catch his death if I don't do something.'

'Better to catch your death than to lift a finger on the Sabbath, as it says in the Book of Proverbs,' Uncle Zech intoned.

'Book of Proverbs, my eye. You've just made it up. I had to learn the Book of Proverbs when we did the Torah Hour at school. I know what's in it and what isn't in it, so don't you start preaching at me!' She ran on, in full flood, 'If it's the Book of Proverbs you're wanting, how about, "A good wife, who can find?" You'll be looking for one if you go on in this vein.'

'"Better to eat raw vegetables in silence, than a sumptuous feast with a sour woman." You can't dispute that's in Proverbs!'

'I'm not sour, I just want to change my baby,' Auntie wailed. 'And don't talk to me about silence. You've treated me to nine surly months of it. I'd have gone mad if it hadn't been for Miriam coming to stay. You're almost as bad as Yahweh, all this taciturn brooding.'

'Thou shalt not take the name of Yahweh in vain,' Uncle lectured.

I heard the sound of a pot smashing against the wall. 'I wasn't taking his name in vain. I was just listing his characteristics. And don't tell me there's an admonition against pot-throwing on the Sabbath, or I'll throw another one at you!'

'Now come on, be reasonable!' said Auntie, adopting a softer, sweeter tone. 'If one of your precious sheep fell down a gully on the Sabbath, you wouldn't think twice about rescuing it. So why can't I rescue my son?'

It was getting like Prime Minister's question time, except that the House of Commons doesn't have a baby's rising shrieks to top off the proceedings. Taking my own cue from the Book of Proverbs, 'She who meddles in another's quarrel is like a woman who grabs a passing dog by the ears,' I marched into the bedroom, picked up the baby out of his cot, washed and changed him in the kitchen, and returned him, dry and sweetly smelling.

Uncle and Auntie watched all this in stunned silence, mouths agape. 'The Sabbath is made for man, not man for the Sabbath,' I quipped, with a sweet smile, before making a strategic exit.

~ Monday 28 June ~

'Oi, oi, oi!' In my dreams I thought Auntie Liz was giving birth again, until I woke up and realized she and Uncle were having another row. 'Leave the child alone, Zech, let him sleep. Let me sleep, too. I'm the one who's been up most of the night with him.'

The sounds of the shuffling steps of an old man suggested that Uncle was pacing the boards around his son's cot. His speech was laboured, the voice the rabbis employ when they are schooling a particularly slow child in Hebrew in preparation for his bar mitzvah: 'Now come on, John, repeat after me, "Repent ye, for the kingdom of heaven is at hand!"'

'Oi, oi, oi, let him be, for goodness sake! You're a year too early teaching him to talk, thirty years too early with that blurb.' Auntie was obviously feeling frayed – she wasn't the only one.

'But I want the message to soak into him from the very start. I'm sure he can understand – he smiled just then.'

'Burped, more likely. Sing that Benedictus to him again and lull us all back to sleep!'

Serenaded by Uncle Zech's dulcet tenor, we all returned to slumber:

> In the tender compassion of our Yahweh,
> the dawn from on high shall break upon us,
> to shine on those who dwell in darkness
> and the shadow of death:
> and to guide our feet into the way of peace.

Whatever you say about the Book of Common Prayer, they don't write lyrics like that any more.

~ Thursday 1 July ~

The internecine strife generated by Uncle and Auntie having their staid old age interrupted by parenthood is getting to me. To give me a break, Luke steals me off to London again. This time we go to a theatre, another type of church, to see the show *Evita*, billed as 'From tart to saint in one lifetime'. I was quite enjoying all the action until Luke whispered, 'Who does Eva remind you of?'

'Well, she's a bit like my Auntie Judith when she still had her figure, otherwise I can think of no one in particular.'

'Look under your nose, then,' Luke advised. 'The lyrics are trying to parallel her with you.'

My hackles rose as Eva trilled, 'I'm a new age Madonna with a golden touch!' She wasn't like me in the slightest. In fact, she's a dead ringer for Bathsheba, who worked her way up from being the wife of a lowly Hittite to being Queen of Israel. A bit of strategic roof-bathing near the royal palace caught the king's eye, and she never looked back, becoming Queen Mother of Israel's wisest king, divider of babies and author of proverbs galore. Now there's a story to catch the imagination.

'Well, maybe,' Luke agreed, when I told him. 'But somehow I don't see "I'm a new age Bathsheba with a golden touch" grabbing them in quite the same way. You've got to come to terms with the fact that from now on, you're going to set the world's trend, Miriam. Art, sculpture, music, fashion, theatre, pop, theology, worship, nuns: all are going to look to your lead. Or the lead they project onto you, forged by their prejudices, fears and failings.'

That's the trouble with doctors: they get so serious sometimes. It was a silly show, anyway. Fancy expecting your gullible audience to believe that world leaders and revolutionaries suddenly burst into song. I put on a superior air as I burst forth with the Magnificat.

~ *Sunday 4 July* ~

To give Auntie quality time with her new babe, Dr Luke decrees that we need to get Uncle Zech out of the house: His constant bickering is wearing her down. I feign interest in Uncle's priestly activities and implore him to show me round the temple. My little girl look, wide-eyed with head fawning slightly to one side, works a treat. Suspending his paternity leave, he volunteers for the duty rota and off we gallop. Although gallop is perhaps an exaggeration, considering the dilatory nature of Uncle's ass.

We approach Jerusalem by the Jericho road. By the roadside a man lay groaning, bloody and bruised, his clothes torn and scattered by bandits who had mugged him for every drachma. Uncle digs his heels hard into his ass's belly, and we positively rush by. 'Uncle, that man needed help,' I cry.

'I'm sure he did. But we've got to get a move on if I'm going to make the evening sacrifice,' Uncle Zech explained. 'And besides, he was as good as dead. Just touch a dead man and you're instantly defiled. No point in coming back to work only to be barred from temple service before you even begin. I had a hard enough time convincing them that being near a woman in childbirth hadn't made me unclean. Why do you think they give us paternity leave?'

Even so, his words rang hollow. I turned my ass to go to the aid of the wounded man, but Uncle pulled me back, 'Don't be stupid, Miriam. You saw what those bandits did to him. Just use your imagination and think what they'd do to you. You've got too much at stake than to meet your end here, a dead rag by the wayside.'

Uncle spat, as if to emphasize his point. But then I twigged that he wasn't spitting at me, but at a hated Samaritan, passing by us as he headed towards Jericho. 'Let's hope the bandits do to him what they did to that poor Jew. That would be no more than he or his kin deserves. The only good Samaritan is a dead Samaritan.' Uncle Zech's words came out like venom. We Jews are indeed a hard people.

I sobbed for the wounded man. I imagined a wife looking out anxiously for her husband, children looking out
anxiously for their daddy – a husband, a father who would
never arrive to comfort them. I sobbed for the Samaritan,
for the irreconcilable bitterness between peoples of different
race and creed. 'Yahweh, does it have to be like this, so cruel,
so unremittingly cruel?'

For once, Yahweh replied. 'I know, Miriam, I know. Let's
see what we can do to rewrite the story.'

~ Monday 5 July ~

Talk about passive smoking! The smells of incense, burning
lamb-fat and smouldering dove-flesh fill the temple. Believe
me, the fog's thicker than the one which ground London to
a halt in 1952 and heralded the Clean Air Act. We need its
ecclesiastical equivalent in this place. What's more, some
under-arm deodorant wouldn't come amiss – the rancid
pong of too many people in too hot a climate really turns
my stomach. Which reminds me – the pregnancy sickness
has stopped.

~ Tuesday 6 July ~

There he stood, in the middle of the temple precincts,
immaculately dressed with not a hair out of place (unless
you've got a thing against dreadlocks), barraging poor old
Yahweh with a running commentary. Now I know where
John Betjeman got the idea for his prattling woman in 'In
Westminster Abbey'.

'Oh Yahweh, I thank you that you have made me to be
such a religious man. I give away 20 per cent of my income
to charity, when 10 per cent is the norm. On two days a

week, I eat nothing because of my love for your law. You know all too well we only have to fast on one day per week, but I thought you'd be pleased if your gracious servant gave you a little bit extra.'

'A right little Jack Horner we've got here,' I thought to myself.

But then his tone became quite vehement, almost spitting in the way Uncle Zech did at the Samaritan, 'I thank you, Lord, that you've made me good and pure and holy, that you've kept me separate from the riff-raff, like that Jezebel over there.'

At first I thought he was referring to me. But then I saw her, in the shadows, back to the wall, shoulders hunched, a tiny baby whimpering in her arms. The timid stance jarred with the red dress (which liberally revealed her charms), the tresses of auburn hair, the heavy make-up. Here was a harlot in trouble, if that's not tautologous. Eyes downcast, she wailed, 'Oh Yahweh, have mercy on me, a sinner.'

'Yahweh, I thank you that you have no truck with women like her,' Jack Horner ranted on. 'I thank you that she and her kind are bound for Hades and everlasting torment. I thank you that you have set me, your servant, for paradise.'

'In your dreams, Pharisee!' I went over to the woman, put my arm around her and we shared a holy silence.

~ Wednesday 7 July ~

To cure myself of temple claustrophobia, I go for an early morning walk to the east of the city, a scramble down through the Kidron valley and then a steep, exhilarating climb up the Mount of Olives. As I sit down amongst the gnarled timeless trees to get my breath back, I gaze over the city, and wonder.

Being moved by the glory of it all is quickly replaced by another feeling. I begin to shiver. Not just because of the cold morning air, but with sheer terror, dread at what lies ahead. What on earth am I doing, going along with all this? How can I, or my yet-to-be-born son, ever hope to make even the slightest impact on this religious system, so tightly sewn up as to brook no intrusion, no alteration. This factory of religion will chew us up and spew us out, grinding relentlessly on as it always has and always will, with not a thought for people like me. Oh Yahweh, let's forget all about it!

Yahweh is surprisingly upbeat. 'This is to be a fresh start, Miriam, an end to all the hypocrisy and religious posturing. Through you and our baby, I want people to know that I'm into everything, all the squalor, all the heartbreaks, all the pain, all the pregnancy sickness, that nothing in all creation is beyond my reach. That's incarnation, girl! I want to abolish the sacred by shouting out that everything is sacred!'

'A laudable ambition,' I reply. 'As a sermon, that deserves a straight alpha. But doesn't it seem a funny way to go about it, kicking off the Yahweh's-Into-Everything-Show with a virgin birth. It does give the teeniest weeniest impression that you ain't into sex.'

'Oh no, I passionately believe that with delight and tenderness couples may know each other through love. After all, it says so in the Alternative Service Book. But we had to go for a virginal conception so I could put my signature to the venture from the start. No more or no less than that. Don't worry, Miriam, I won't let you down. We'll win through. Remember that I am with you.'

Remembering Yahweh's with me makes me shake even more with terror. With a heavy heart I retrace my steps down the hillside. By the time I reach the brook of Kidron a total weariness envelops me and I sit down and weep. I am startled out of my grief by a stray donkey, who nuzzles against me and won't leave my side. I climb onto her cross-marked back, and together we ride into Jerusalem.

~ Thursday 8 July ~

I never would have believed it, but I found myself craving for a pizza. I guess it's a reaction to all that Judean lamb. As if it wasn't enough gorging ourselves on it morning, noon and night up on the moors, we have it burnt to a cinder in the temple precincts to boot. If I was into Freudian analysis (actually I prefer Jung), I suppose I would see the pizza as a symbol of home, round, soft, maternal, something I yearn to return to deep down. I don't have to go very deep down to remember home as it really was – the ballistic pans, the tirade of abuse from Momma. I certainly don't miss that.

But I do miss Galilee, such a contrast to here, this sweating, sick and hot place. I long to slake my thirst there, in Gennesaret's clear brooks, to rest beneath the vine and fig trees' shadow, to gaze delightfully on the waving corn, the gleaming lilies, the distant mountains.

I have to admit I cribbed all that flowery stuff from a piece of Victorian romance, extolling the Holy Land's attractions. The writer doesn't mention the small-minded population, the stone-throwing youths, the prohibitive price of olive oil. Still, it's nice to dream.

~ Friday 9 July ~

I suppose these dreams are fuelled by Rupert Brooke, my poet of the week. I've said before how I spend a lot of my time brooding over the battlefields of the Great War –

their sheer futility wrings out my heart. It strikes me that it must be a very primitive religion which sacrifices so many of its sons in such a bloody way. At least Yahweh (admittedly with his customary trait of popping up at the fifty-ninth second of the fifty-ninth minute of the eleventh hour) pulled Abraham back from the brink when he was going to quarter his only son, Isaac. Isaac in Hebrew means laughter, but there weren't a lot of laughs in that incident, let me tell you. Not a lot of laughs in the Great War either. Why was the twentieth century so deaf to Yahweh's cry to draw back from the carnage?

I saw Brooke sacrificed in the Mediterranean, in yet another ill-fated campaign in a war of ill-fated campaigns. But as far as ill-fatedness went, this campaign took the biscuit, with its architect, the First Lord of the Admiralty, forced to resign, a rare event in the Great War. Winston Churchill was his name. Now I'm sure I've come across him again somewhere on my sojourns into the future, but can't for the life of me remember where.

Anyway, Brooke was gorgeous: He had a tremendous beauty about him that made my girl's heart race. It angered me to see him snuffed out, at a whim. In grief I trawled through his poetry, and found him there, alive and immortal.

Some of his poems are retrospectively sad, naively extolling the warfare which robbed him of life itself. But my favourite poem, which catches my home-sickness to a tee, was written before the war. On holiday in Germany and oppressed by an urbane Berlin, Brooke longed for his native Grantchester, epitome of the Fens and Jeffrey Archer: 'Here I am, sweating, sick and hot, and there the shadowed waters fresh lean up to embrace the naked flesh . . .'

You can see why he catches my plight. Εἴθε γενοιμην – would I were in Galilee . . . So I search out the Pizza Casa, order myself a St Peter Fish and Fig special, and savour the tastes of home.

~ Saturday 10 July ~

The Sabbath gives me time to reflect on my last supper. In my experience pizzas never live up to their promise, but what made the evening memorable was the company and not the food.

The Casa was packed with Roman soldiers. Apparently every night in July they party, toasting Julius Caesar, the emperor who, understandably piqued by the Ides of March, conferred his name on this month instead. There was just one table spare, in a quietish corner by the kitchens, where I sat alone and surveyed the scene.

I wasn't alone for long. She was a little older than me, jet-black hair in braids, ivory skin, ruby-red lips. 'Do you think I could join you?' she anxiously asked. 'I find all these soldiers so threatening. We girls have to stick together, don't we?'

Since (as I've mentioned before) all the soldiers garrisoned in this backwater are gay, I didn't share her fears. It was Josiah the waiter, rather than us girls, who had to watch himself when Romans were around.

Even so, it was good to have some company to distract me from home-sickness, so I slid my pizza plate along and made room for her. We hit it off straight away.

Like me, she hated all the hypocrisy and sham which oozed out of every holy wall in this religious place. She too would have tenderly comforted the shamed woman I felt so sorry for in the temple. Like me, she yearned for an end to the violence, to the unnecessary killing which has been the Holy Land's trademark since the Garden of Eden's tenancy fell vacant. Like me, she hated all the wealth wasted, squandered on arms, frittered away on religious bric-a-brac. 'Just think how many poor people could be fed for a year with the money it takes to run the temple for one day,' she confided.

Like me, she hated mozzarella cheese, the elastic streaks which stretched between your plate and fork and mouth, stubbornly sticking to your chin and bosom, defying any attempt to eat delicately. Considering the galaxy of foods banned as unclean under the law given us on Sinai, I'm surprised Moses turned a blind eye to mozzarella. The manufacturers probably secured his bias by naming it after him. Although how a cheese called 'Little Moses' could ever be successfully marketed defeats me.

The conversation flowed, and by the early hours we were firm friends. I promised to look her up whenever I visited Jerusalem. She insisted on paying for the whole meal, explaining that she had just won a massive thirty pieces of silver on the lottery roll-over. Josiah, the much ogled waiter, was embarrassed by the size of the tip, 'Oh Mrs Iscariot, you shouldn't, you know!'

I skipped towards the dawn, my home-sickness banished, feeling I had found a loyal friend for life.

~ Monday 12 July ~

Speaking of loyal friends, Luke pops up and takes me a short ride from Jerusalem to Bethany to meet a family he's especially fond of. They have three children all under five, and Luke thinks it would be good for me to have a glimpse of what the pre-school years hold in store. Just in case I didn't have enough to worry about giving birth to the Son of God, I now have to fret over what Jesus will be like when he goes through the terrible two's.

In the event, the family entertain us lavishly, and I'm very taken with the children. All three of them are absolute darlings, yet amazingly their characters are so different from each other. Four-year-old Martha, the oldest, is the organizer and never ceases to be busy, helping her momma in the kitchen, washing the dishes, stoking the stove, fluffing up the cushions in the living room, picking up the traces of mud dropped from our dirty feet. During the three hours we stayed there, she never stopped buzzing around.

Unlike her sister and my namesake, three-year-old Miriam. She just sat on a cushion, still for the whole three hours, listening to Luke with wide-open eyes, soaking in what he had to say. Martha kept making cutting remarks about it being all right for some people who could spend their days lolling around on cushions, but Miriam was happily oblivious to it all.

Two-year-old Lazarus was a tyke, scaling cliff faces, crawling into caves, getting stuck in dark tunnels. Just before we arrived, he had had a fall and gashed his head. Luke bandaged it expertly, sternly advising him to take it easy. But as soon as our backs were turned, he was off, scrambling into a cave. 'Lazarus, come forth!' Luke bellowed. At his command, the little lad came strolling nonchalantly out, bandage in disarray, a broad grin on his face which proved contagious and made us all chuckle. Even the ever-busy Martha's lips twitched with the hint of a smile. 'Ee, that boy's antics will be the death of us, you mark my words,' she chided, old before her time.

~ Saturday 17 July ~

Uncle's tour of duty completed, we've come back to the farm. Auntie has had the chance to get a routine established with her new babe, Uncle has been reminded of his horizons, so the whole place has a better feel. So Dr Luke's prescription worked a treat.

The one thing you're allowed to do on the Sabbath is read. You remember our visit to the religious bookshop in London, when I thumbed through all the mad theses about me? Well, I was also rather taken with a tome of poetry written by a priest who hangs around in the extremities of Wales, not all that different from me hanging around in the wilds of Judea. R. S. Thomas is his name, or R. S. Twin if you translate it back into Greek.

He catches the bleakness of the human condition with a perception which makes your heart stop. He is ruthlessly honest about faith – no sham, no pretence, no playing the Pharisee. He rings bells with me, and that's why I keep returning to him.

A lot of his poetry is puzzling, impenetrable, but then a brilliant line leaps out of the page at you and you say, 'Aha, I see!' I spend the Sabbath flipping through those best lines.

He writes about a barn owl, an abomination screeching in the wilderness according to our purity laws. But don't take too much notice of that, since most of us, according to our purity laws, are an abomination. Thomas likens the owl's haunting cry to 'the voice of God in the darkness, cursing himself fiercely for his lack of love'. That sounds like my Yahweh.

Another favourite bit is where he describes a pilgrimage where God proves maddeningly elusive, 'such a fast God, always before us and leaving as we arrive'. Gandalf-like Yahweh rides again.

'The meaning is in the waiting', Thomas tells me. Don't I know it: nine long months of waiting for Yahweh's final word. An expectant mother, looking forward to the time of birth, almost wishing the before-time away. Yet perhaps there is meaning in the waiting which is worth dwelling on: the sickness; the rejection; this wilderness – all part and parcel of the revelation, themselves pregnant with significance to pregnant old me.

And the waiting itself speaks powerfully to me. When the lynch mob (or rather the stone mob) threw me at Joe's door, it seemed as if eternity stood still, poised in the balance, as I waited for death or life, to be repulsed or to be accepted. A painful, hopeful waiting . . .

The poem I love most paints a rural picture: an old farmer, nearing death, fearing for his own future and the world he is about to leave. But his despair is turned around when he sees, in the distance, his grandson ploughing. 'His young wife fetches him cakes and tea and a dark smile. It is well.'

I give Yahweh a dark smile on this Sabbath Day. All shall be well, and all shall be well and all manner of thing shall be well: Words I whisper to Mother Julian of Norwich to brighten her medieval gloom.

~ Monday 19 July ~

'Now, Esther's grandma, Rebecca, she has a sister called Susannah who's married to a chap called Jonathan, who's the uncle of Zach's cousin Lot . . .' Auntie Liz was giving me a very convoluted explanation as to why she, Uncle, baby John, Dr Luke and I were all wobbling on our asses over the hills, bound for Esther's wedding. Trying to work out my precise relationship to the bride made me reel.

By the time we reached the Jerusalem by-pass I gave up

trying, and did some integral calculus in my head, far less taxing on the brain.

One thing was certain: We were very distant relatives indeed of Esther, so why were we invited to the do? 'It's a complicated story,' Auntie Liz began. Why is it that nothing we Israelis get up to is ever simple? 'Well, Esther's father, Mahershalalhashbaz . . .'

'Maherwhat?' I asked, incredulous.

Mahershalalhashbaz,' Uncle Zech broke in. 'I thought you'd have know that, Miriam,' he scolded. 'He was one of Isaiah the prophet's children. You can look it up in Isaiah 8.3 when we get home.'

'Anyway,' Auntie Liz continued, tutting at her husband's interruption, 'Mahershalalhashbaz is a power in the land, owner-manager of a multi-national wine company with vineyards in Greece, France, Spain and Scotland as well as Israel.'

'Scotland?' I asked, with a puzzled frown. 'I didn't know they had vineyards in Scotland?'

'No dear, they don't. To be honest, Scotland was a mistake. Cousin Baz was seduced by the prospect of a cheap workforce. But any vines which grew in the cold climate proved puny. And the workforce, though certainly cheap, was mostly absent. They either had a hangover from drinking the local firewater they produce in massive quantities, or they were prone to take weeks off at a time, demolishing stone walls the Romans had erected. But he soon put Scotland behind him, since the rest of the firm is booming. It's all to do with size, you see.'

I giggled as Auntie raised her eyebrows and gave me a mischievous look. Uncle Zech frowned at us sharply, but Auntie took no notice and continued unabated, a veritable Fawlty Towers Sybil undeterred by a crusty Basil. 'The company's success is due in no small part to the wine coming in such generously sized bottles – they have to be big enough to get the name Mahershalalhashbaz on the label.'

'At least in that respect, Cousin Baz has got the advantage on his rival firm, run by his hated brother Shear-jashub.'

'Isaiah 7,' Uncle quipped before I had had time to query yet another odd name. Clearly their parents must have had a thing about Isaiah.

'To be honest, all the wine tastes the same to me,' Auntie admitted. 'But don't let Cousin Baz hear me say that. He and Shear-jashub are at each other's throats day in, day out. Shear-jashub has just head-hunted and poached thirty of Cousin Baz's most experienced regional managers, which meant that thirty names which were on Esther's wedding list are now on Cousin Baz's hit list.'

'That's all very interesting, Auntie,' I lied, stifling a yawn. 'But I still don't get where we come in.'

'Oh come on, Miriam, you're going to have to be a bit sharper with that omniscient son of yours on the way. Cousin Baz is a proud man, and is absolutely determined that his daughter's wedding should be the wedding of the aeon, and that the reception should be full. So he's had to trawl around the reserve lists to bid distant relatives such as us to come to the feast, pretending that he was going to invite us all along.'

'The stone which the builders rejected has become the corner stone,' Uncle Zech intoned. 'The guests which were left out are now let in.' He really is a weird old man, with a line of scripture for every eventuality, making us feel like mere actors moving on Yahweh's tightly scripted stage.

~ Tuesday 20 July ~

On the third day of the week there was a wedding at the

Star of David Inn at Emmaus . . . Why marry on a Tuesday and not a Saturday like any normal couple? Well, first and foremost, on Saturday you wouldn't get the caterers to lift a finger, owing to it being the Sabbath. 'Remember that thou keep holy the Sabbath Day. Six days shalt thou labour and do all the cooking thou hast to do, but the seventh day is the Sabbath of the Lord thy God. In it thou shalt do no manner of work, thou and thy son and thy daughter and thy manservant and thy maidservant and thy cattle, and Abrahams Exquisite Caterers Ltd,' as it says in the Prayer Book, if my memory serves me correct.

So we Jews shifted wedding days to Tuesday, pretending it was traditional anyway. After all Tuesday, the third day, was the only day of creation in Genesis when Yahweh performs a double activity, setting a precedent for the day uniting two into one. As one of Solomon's hidden proverbs goes: 'As Yahweh produced land and vegetables on the third day, so a wedding produces a husband and wife.' Not one of Solomon's best I fear. I guess that's why they hid it away.

~ Wednesday 21 July ~

As we saunter back to Lone Moors Farm, we pick over the cracks in the wedding of the aeon, which, after all, is the traditional activity of every wedding guest since the beginning of time. 'Ee, those bridesmaids,' Auntie Liz chuckled. 'Five of them puddings and five of them as thin as Uncle Zech was on the day of our wedding. Why he had to go and fast for forty days before we got married, I've never quite been able to fathom.'

'I was fasting for the feast beyond, my sweet,' Uncle Zech replied, dewy-eyed. The wedding had obviously stirred up his loins. Or maybe Luke had slipped him another dose of Viagra.

The puddings had proved dull-witted as well as over-weight, and had gone off shopping at the very point they should have led the bride to her new home. The five maids who remained, thin and shrewish, made a sorry sight. Cousin Baz was furious that his darling daughter's bridal procession should look so funeral. When the missing girls eventually shuffled along, expecting pride of place at the reception, he threw them out and bolted the door.

'Well,' Auntie Liz continued, 'If there's one thing that should have gone without a hitch at a Mahershalalhashbaz wedding, it's the wine. Ee, I think it was wicked of those regional managers, sabotaging those dozen cases of Cousin Baz's very best before they cleared their desks and left his employ.'

It was indeed a sorry outcome. They had substituted water for the wine (or at least I hope it was water), so we were condemned to a dry wedding. By the time replacement cases had been fetched from the depot in Jerusalem, the party was well nigh over.

In all the confusion, Esther lost one of the ten gold coins presented to her by Jacob, her new husband, as her bride price. Not a wealthy man, Jacob had toiled and scraped to raise the money, toiled and scraped for love. Given the coin's sentimental value, Esther was understandably hysteria-stricken. 'Oi, oi, oi!' she wailed, obviously a mandatory formula for all Jewish women immersed in grief. Little wonder that we Jewish girls get such a bad deal, when our vocabulary of sorrow is so impoverished.

To cheer her up, we all sank to our knees and grovelled as we sifted the dust and sundry debris amassed in the 100 per cent bulrush matting. Colliding with unfamiliar guests beneath trestle tables was certainly a novel way of breaking the ice. I bumped heads with a young man with piercing blue eyes, who was breaking up a discarded bread bun to see if the coin lurked there. I had never met him before, and yet *déjà vu* was ringing in my ears. I had this strange sensation that I had known him all my days. I looked again, and he was gone from my sight.

As I panned the room searching for him, a glint of gold caught my eye. 'Eureka!' I cried, showing off my classical education as I held the shiny coin up high. The whole room cheered as the colour returned to Esther's cheeks and the light to her eyes. Sometimes it's quite fun being the Mediatrix.

'It was the wedding of the aeon, all right,' quipped the ever garrulous Auntie Liz. 'But not for the reasons Cousin Baz had in mind. All those cock-ups will certainly be the gossip of Palestine for generations to come. Maybe even part of our folklore. Write it down, Luke, you like recording things. Yahweh knows, we need a little light relief from all that angel of death and blood of the lamb stuff.'

~ Thursday 22 July ~

I awoke from a strange dream. In it my yet-to-be born child had grown up into manhood and had formed his own wine multi-national to rival the feuding companies of Shear-jashub's and Mahershalalhashbaz's, soon outrunning both of them. He had named his firm after Isaiah's third child, coining the slogan, 'Emmanuel, wine for the world.' His health was toasted daily in elaborate drinking rituals throughout the world, with inn after inn bearing his name. The inns were queer, decorous places, neither public houses nor synagogues, yet containing elements of both. Although business was clearly booming, there was also an impoverished streak: Each inn only had one cup to share between the whole crowd.

59

Weird, impossible dreams. Having goat's cheese for supper makes for dangerous nights.

~ Saturday 24 July ~

Strange feelings within me today, like butterflies fluttering in my womb. Dr Luke forewarned me about them: My unborn child is beginning to stir. Hush, little one, don't you know that even such work as movement is forbidden on the Sabbath?

~ Friday 6 August ~

My unborn babe now reminds me of his presence virtually every hour. It's a strange sensation, being kicked in the ribs by Yahweh's final revelation. Although, if you read our scriptures, you'll realize that Yahweh's done a fair bit of kicking in his time: We Jews are not so much God's chosen people as his kicked people. Though I've got this funny feeling, judging by Yahweh's tenderness of late, that father-hood will mellow him.

I'm in the holiday feel, so Luke and I go on tour: Masada, Herod's fortress overlooking the Dead Sea. Herod has fallen on hard times recently, so he's opened up all his palaces at weekends to members of the public, with a swingeing three drachma entry fee per head. Since it was the very taxes of the members of the public which paid for Herod's palaces in the first place, my fellow countrymen are not too fussed at being charged twice over, and so tend to steer clear. And given Herod's murderous track record, the term 'per head' when applied to entering one of his strongholds hardly encourages punters.

Before making the steep ascent, we cool ourselves off by

bathing in the Dead Sea, taking care to keep our sandals on so as not to cut ourselves on the debris on the shore. Really, you'd think these Roman soldiers would have learnt by now to take their litter home with them, rather than dump it here. I sometimes wonder whether the sole purpose of their mighty Empire is to provide waste disposal far from Italy's shores.

And the Dead Sea is a rubbish tip *par excellence*, since everything flows in, but nothing whatsoever flows out. Unlike my beloved Galilee, where waters come and go and freshness reigns. Maybe you only teem with life when you let go rather than hold on.

The sheer climb to Masada was the best work-out I'd had all year. Muscles throbbed where hitherto I didn't even know I had muscles, my breaths had to be drawn deep and frequently, the exhilaration meant that every colour (not that there's that much colour around the Dead Sea) was bathed in dazzling light. 'Are you sure a girl in my condition ought to be doing this?' I asked Luke.

'Don't whine, it'll do you good,' Luke replied, with the typical curtness of the medical profession. He's tremendously liberal when it comes to ante-natal care.

As anticipated, we have the place virtually to ourselves. The views are just out of this world, although the castle isn't up to very much. The soldiers-turned-guides do their best, go out of their way to be polite, but apart from pointing out the ramparts and bulwarks and stinking garderobes, there's not much else they can do. They stare dewy-eyed over the wasted desert and poisoned sea and say, 'It's worth being here, just for the view.' I knew that already.

Even Herod himself makes an appearance, dressed in his weekend tweeds – a trifle hot for this climate, I would have thought, judging by the sweat that pours off him. He goes out of his way to be genial, asking Luke about his work and patients, making cooing noises about me being pregnant, enquiring when the baby is due and where I plan to give birth . . . Despite the intense heat, compounded by our hard climb, a sudden chill fills my soul with dread.

After this exchange of pleasantries, Herod gives his apologies, 'Do excuse me, but I've got my boxes to attend to.'

'Of course,' we demur. Once he has departed, I begin to thaw. My baby gives me a massive kick in celebration. Even taciturn old Yahweh feels moved to chip in a comment, 'That's my boy, Miriam.'

~ *Part Three* ~

~ Sunday 15 August ~

It's time to return to Nazareth. I've been stuck here in Judea long enough and I can't hide myself away for ever. Luke rides by my side, just in case there is any trouble. Although he assures me that most of the local louts are now far away, serving in manoeuvres with the Zealot Resistance, channelling their energies into throwing stones at the Romans rather than me.

The roads are uncannily quiet, with not a fish caravan to be seen. Usually it's so busy that camels are tail-gating each other, bearing fish caught in the fresh waters of my Lake Galilee to be delivered to a hungry Jerusalem, sick to the teeth of lamb with everything. The inhabitants of Jerusalem are also sick to the teeth that the only nearby lake they can muster is the sulphurous Dead Sea we visited last week: Good for curing eczema, not so good for yielding fish. A barren lake on top of too much lamb goes in some way to explain all their angst. Supplying them with our local Galilean delicacy restores their diet's balance and calms the hyperactivity for which Jerusalem residents are renowned.

On a hot day, road travel is best avoided; the stench of fish makes you retch. There is a lot of concern about fish pollution and the effect it's having on the weather. More squalls at sea, earthquakes, shooting stars, global warming, you know the sort of thing. You can always find some expert out to make a name for himself by blaming it all on the ozone given off by rotting fish.

'Why is it so quiet?' I asked Luke, fearing an ambush lurking by the wayside. My memory of that poor wounded man which Uncle and I passed by on the Jerusalem road was still sharp and painful.

'It's the Jerusalem Works' Fortnight, Miriam, that's why no one is around. The weather's far too hot at this time of the year to transport fish, so they're all having a break, holidaying in some exotic clime.'

Luke looked pensive, before he added, 'The thought's just occurred to me that in centuries to come, most of Catholic Europe will close down on this day too. And all because of you, Miriam.'

'Why?' I asked. 'What on earth am I going to do that'll bring the whole world to a halt?'

'You're going to be assumed,' Luke explained.

'Not if I can avoid it,' I snap. It sounds like another pre-natal test that Luke has dreamt up. 'Surely not another examination; you only checked me out last week, and said everything was just fine.'

'It is fine. No, your Assumption is decades away. Instead of dying, you're going to be transported, body and soul, straight into heaven. Without even a whiff of corruption. Catholic Europe will be given the day off to celebrate. In fact it's a wonder Catholic Europe gets any work done at all, given all the feast days you're going to shower on them: your annunciation, your visitation, your birthday, your conception day, your son's birthday, the day of your purification . . .'

'But I'm not sure I fancy all that,' I interrupted. 'Why can't I have a decent death, like everyone else?'

'Because you're a star, Miriam. How many times do I have to tell you? Look at the effect Princess Diana's dying had. You'll upstage even her, because you're not just going to die. All stars are assumed, simply disappear without a trace. Just think of the heroes of our faith: Moses, Elijah, Enoch, . . .'

'And Glenn Miller, Lord Lucan, and Shergar, I suppose!' I quip. 'I'm not sure I want to be lumped with that lot.'

'Oh, forget the twentieth century,' Luke advised. 'By then they're really scratching around for heroes. Just remember that you'll be the all-time-tops. You're the prima donna of the select bunch who'll walk around Elysium's golden fields with your terrestrial legs still intact.'

'Well, let's just hope that once I've given birth, my legs return to normal,' I shrug. Putting up with varicose veins for all eternity strikes me as a funny sort of laurel.

~ Monday 16 August ~

Noon: Arrive in Nazareth. The welcome is muted, fortunately. Just one consumptive youth, too feeble to be conscripted by the Zealots. He manages to summon up sufficient energy to hurl a few pieces of gravel my way, but they all fall short. Exhausted by his efforts, he slinks away, too drained to shout any abuse.

Momma is all over me. 'To think, my darling daughter is to bear Yahweh's Son. I always knew you were cut out for greatness. The chosen one of the chosen people! Miriam, pray remember your tender momma when you come into your kingdom.'

The definite lisp in her delivery betrays the angelic source for her change of heart. I'm not sure I can cope with all this gush. I'm already yearning for flying pizza pans.

~ Tuesday 17 August ~

Spend the morning helping in the kitchen, being fussed over by Momma. 'Now don't you knead that dough too vigorously, Miriam. Remember that you've got the Maker of the stars and sea becoming a child within you!' I could kill that angel for showing her John Betjeman's Christmas poem. As Momma kneads the dough, she chants rhythmically and incessantly, 'And is it true, and is it true, and is it true...' A bit of a non-question when your divinely pregnant daughter is rolling pastry beside you.

~ Wednesday 18 August ~

Sneak over to Joe's house to get a break from pizzas, Momma and Betjeman. Find my intended puzzling over an unusual summons which he received in this morning's mail. Under the new self-assessment tax system, everyone has to register at the birth place of their ancestors. Not very logical, I grant you, but when, since the dawn of creation, has the Inland Revenue ever tried to be logical? Joe and I are bound for the tiny village of Bethlehem, because he is of the house and lineage of David by descent.

Mind you, the way my hero David carried on (just read 1 and 2 Samuel behind closed doors in a plain paper cover and prepare to be shocked), I should think nearly everyone in Israel is of the house and lineage of David by descent, so Bethlehem will have some traffic queue on 25 December, the day of the summons...

~ Sunday 29 August ~

Dr Luke has persuaded me to join an ante-natal class at nearby Capernaum, run by his friend, Mr Theophilus, a consultant obstetrician and gynaecologist. Mr Theophilus trained Luke and keeps a fatherly eye on him. From time to time, the two men surf the centuries together, on the look out for interesting medical innovations, which is what gave them the idea for the class.

Any notion of preparing for birth is, to say the least, a novelty in these parts. Mrs Jonah, a huge fish-wife of a woman from the shores of Galilee, was openly critical from the start. 'I don't know what we're wasting our time here for, being instructed in how to give birth, as if we didn't know already. You just hitch up your skirts, drop your sprog and then get on with your work, like any other woman since the dawn of creation. We've got fishing nets to mend – we can't waste our time on fine talk about birth techniques.'

'Madam,' Mr Theophilus replied, looking her straight in the eye, unruffled by her brusque manner. 'We're all on the same side, we all want to make birth as simple as possible. But a third of women die in labour in this primitive land. All this class aims to do is to enable you to live to see your baby grow up.'

His Greek had a cut-glass accent which commanded respect, and made even Mrs Jonah silent for a while. But when he started demonstrating how wailing during labour could control the pain (with a predictable 'Oi, oi, oi'), Mrs Jonah could constrain herself no more. 'Mr Theophilus,' she boomed. 'I can assure you that I do not cry out in labour, neither did my mother before me nor her mother before her. To cry out would be beneath our dignity. We've suffered stoically in silence for generations. Even if every other woman here cried out, I can assure you I would not cry out. I would rather die.'

Not wishing to step out of line with their self-appointed shop steward, all the other women were quick to say the same, with only shy old me remaining silent. 'Let me assure you, Mrs Jonah, before cockcrow on the very night of your labour you will have cried out at least three times,' Mr Theophilus pronounced, with a prophetic chill in his voice. Surfing the future obviously has its perks when it comes to predicting your patients' medical history.

'What you going to call yours then?' Mrs Jonah bawled at me over a glass of Mahershalalhashbaz's afterwards. 'Not that there's much of him yet, I can hardly tell you've fallen pregnant,' she added, with the obvious disdain of a gross woman for a slim one.

'Jesus,' I replied.

'A safe choice. It's a good idea to go for the commonplace. A name like that will never be out of fashion.'

'And what are you going to call yours?' I asked, returning the compliment.

'Simon, probably. Although the way the solid little beggar slams into my insides when he moves around, I feel like calling him Peter, Rock. But I can't see a name like that ever taking off!'

~ Wednesday 8 September ~

My birthday. Uncle Zech and Auntie Liz sent me a bunch of rather wilted looking roses. Obviously they hadn't travelled well all the way from Judea. I hate roses anyway. I normally suffer from hayfever, and to make matters worse their perfume had a habit of triggering my pregnancy sickness. My dislike of roses is a bit ironic, considering the millions of future devotees who'll place bunch after bunch of them before statues of me scattered throughout the globe in centuries to come. You'd have thought they'd have noticed the statues' red noses and streaming eyes and taken the hint.

Momma and Poppa gave me a card with Happy Hanukkah scrolled on the front; they'd crossed out 'Hanukkah' and replaced it with 'Birthday'. You see, the problem is, you can't get any cards other than Hanukkah cards at this time of the year, the festival being so commercialized these days. Would you believe it, right from the beginning of June, when there's still a full six months to go before the end of December when the festival is due, shops are brim-full of Hanukkah candles, Hanukkah oil, Hanukkah everlasting matches, Hanukkah luminous camels . . .

All this big sell loses the religious significance. I have to admit I'm not that sure what it all means and how it started, which is a bit rich when I'm carrying God's Final Word in my womb. It was something to do with a load of Greek invaders trying to blow out God's sanctuary light in the temple. Despite the gales of garlic breath the lamp just wouldn't die, but kept on coming back again and again and again – a sort of divine hybrid of Frank Sinatra and Jeffrey Archer. An omen that Yahweh and Israel would never die, whatever the world threw at them. And so, with the logic for which we Jews are famous, we celebrate that immensity with sheer, unadulterated tackiness.

I really feel that with all this commercialization, it's about time we wiped the slate clean and substituted a holier celebration in place of Hanukkah. For the life of me, I can't think what . . .

~ Sunday 12 September ~

Another session of the ante-natal class at Capernaum. Mr Theophilus has us on all fours, panting like dogs, which he assures us will ease the pain when the contractions come. Not surprisingly, Mrs Jonah has a thing or two to say on that score. 'Just because you're a Gentile dog, doesn't mean us good Jewish girls have to catch your filthy habits,' she guffawed. Both Mr Theophilus and Dr Luke blushed a deep crimson. Sometimes the racism of my fellow countrywomen makes my blood run cold.

Over wine I chatted with a sad little woman, who seemed devoid of any self-confidence whatsoever. 'I just can't accept I'm pregnant, I really can't. Until I see my baby's head, and touch his tiny hands and tiny feet and feel he's real, then I will not believe it. I'm sure it's just that I'm putting on a bit of weight, nothing more than that. I've had such an appetite recently.'

'And what are you going to call your baby?' I asked, re-sorting to a predictable line. To think, Luke encouraged me to come to these classes so I could meet interesting people and stretch my mind. Inducing brain death is more likely.

'Thomas,' she replied, 'But I really doubt there'll ever be a baby at all, I really do.'

My eyelids grew heavy as she whined on and on. I've only been to a couple of classes, and already the tedium is getting to me. I comfort myself that it is only a coincidence of timing that has brought me together with these rather stolid women. Once the birth is over, I will never cross their paths again.

~ *Friday 17 September* ~

I'm confined to barracks today, primarily because the local louts aren't, but are on weekend leave from their Zealot training ground. At siesta time, I popped my head around the front door to check whether all was clear, but a rock missed me by inches. 'Death to harlots!' the man who threw it jeered at me with an American drawl. I guess he'd been caught in a time warp and was intervening in Palestine two thousand years too early.

Cooped up with Momma and her incessant recitation of

Betjeman's poem really gets to me. I decide to have a word with the Maker of the skies and sea. 'Lord, why on earth didn't you stage all this two thousand years on?' I raged. 'By then they'll be far more tolerant of unmarried mothers. In fact in the Third Millennium illegitimacy seems *de rigueur*. Why pull this stunt now in such a repressive place? Even the Puritans seem licentious compared to the narrow-minded louts in this village.'

Yahweh's reply was brief and not exactly comforting, typical of his usual taciturn self. 'Where do you think that spirit of tolerance and acceptance will come from, if not from within you?' As I've said before and will doubtless say again, what makes Yahweh doubly infuriating is that he's always right.

~ Sunday 26 September ~

'Oh, Mr Theophilus, what foods should I be eating to give my little James the best start? Will too much lamb harm him?' The woman gently patted her stomach containing her yet unborn child. Yes, we're back at the ante-natal class once again. I feel like Patrick McGoohan in that cult TV series, *The Prisoner*. Episode after episode he thought he'd got away, only to wake up and find himself incarcerated once more. Mind you, being imprisoned in the lovely confines of Portmeirion with Snowdonia as a backdrop is a lot more preferable to being stuck in a sweaty classroom in a dump like Capernaum.

Anyway, to come back to the present, Mrs Boanerges is having this indepth conversation with Mr Theophilus about how to give her baby a headstart over the rest of our off-spring, making all our blood pressures rise in the process. Hardly the point of these sessions.

'I don't think anyone can have too much lamb...' Mr Theophilus advised.

'You speak for yourself!' I thought.

'...All that iron and protein can only build up your unborn babe.'

'But surely we have to be careful about Mad Ewe disease? We older ones will have caught whatever we're going to catch from it already, but we ought not to expose the young, that's what my husband Zebedee says.'

'Boing!' I think. Why is it that whenever Mrs Boanerges mentions her husband, the *Magic Roundabout* comes to mind? I think I'm watching too much television.

'No, there's no such thing as Mad Ewe Disease,' Mr Theophilus reassured her. 'It's just something dreamt up by fish merchants to promote their product. You ate lamb when you were carrying your son, John. No ill-effects there, are there?'

'Don't you go casting a slur on us fish merchants,' Mrs Jonah interrupted. 'We work hard for a living, put our lives at risk going out in all weathers, braving Galilee's squalls. It's all right for you, with your Gentile ways, all smooth hands and smooth talk...'

Mr Theophilus was saved further embarrassment by Mrs Boanerges' persistence, 'What about drink? Is there anything I should be avoiding?'

'No, as long as you drink in moderation you'll be fine. You can do no better than Mahershalalhashbaz's, so let's take a break and all have a glass,' concluded Mr T., clearly in need of a couple of bottles.

'That Mrs Boanerges never lets up,' Luke commented as we rode home. 'Always wanting the best for her sons, even while they're still in the womb. Do you know, it's not just Theophilus she pesters. She's always on at the rabbi, about how to make sure her boys get the best place in the kingdom of heaven. Where will such neurosis end?'

'Can they drink of the cup that I will drink,' I quip.

'Only if it's filled with Mahershalalhashbaz!' Luke replies, eyes twinkling with amusement. He looks gorgeous when he smiles like that.

~ Tuesday 5 October ~

I find I've totally gone off pizza bread, a bit of a disadvantage for someone who's a skivvy in a pizza parlour. I know, pregnant women are supposed to eat some odd things and get some weird cravings. But instead of the Italian cooking prized by the local militia, I gorge myself on loaves and loaves of flat bread, the more unleavened the better, with sardines sandwiched between each slice. Never mind eating for two, I'm sure I've eaten enough to feed five thousand by now. My taste buds have altered as well – pure Cana sparkling water tastes more like wine these days. If we'd all been afflicted this way at Esther's unfortunately alcohol-free wedding, then Mahershalalhashbaz would have had no worries. And as for the ever-present lamb, which graces virtually every Jewish meal table, I feel full before I even begin to eat.

~ Monday 11 October ~

You could hardly cross the street in Nazareth today, what with all the traffic. Time was when every village shared one ass between the whole population. Now in these more affluent times, every household has at least two asses, which makes for an awful lot of ass clogging up the highway.

We've just had an election in which the New Pharisee

Party swept to power, although they're only puppet rulers with the Romans still pulling the strings. The political term for it all is pax Romana, to be translated as Pax Americana in a couple of millennia. The Minister for Transport (nick-named the Mouth of the Jordan because he's MP for Jericho) is brimming with useless initiatives, such as the Jerusalem Park and Ride policy, doomed, like the doctrine of predestination, from the very start. The big idea was to park your ass at Bethany in the Jerusalem suburbs, and then take a communal elephant into the city centre. It caused a riot among the high priests when a whole load of elephants deposited more than their human cargo outside the temple gates, so after that the idea was scrapped.

Just imagine what it'll be like in December with every-body's ass, including mine, Joseph's and Dr Luke's heading for Bethlehem. Never mind T. S. Eliot's three magi having a cold coming of it. A cold coming of it we'll be having, with a hundred mile ass back-up out of Judea. Especially when you remember that the whole of Israel is only seventy miles long to start with!

~ *Sunday 17 October* ~

She must have filched the scalpel from the little black bag Dr Luke takes with him everywhere. We were all lying on exercise mats, pedalling our legs in the air to tone up flabby tummy muscles, when she struck. She pulled Mrs Alphaeus to her feet, applied an arm lock and dragged her into a corner, where she pressed the scalpel against her throat. The blade was sharp, scratching the skin's surface, so that a drop of blood trickled a course down her neck. A trailer for what was to come, if Susannah Zealotes lived up to her spiel.

'Death to collaborators!' Susannah exclaimed, her eyes

clear, shining with the wildness of a fanatic. 'No mercy for those in league with Rome! No mercy for those who pass the fruits of our soil over to a foreign power. This is our land, promised us by Yahweh at Sinai for our children and our children's children!'

Luke was amazingly calm. 'Thank you, Susannah, but I'm already well acquainted with the Zealot Party manifesto. And this is a clinic, not a political convention – medicine and politics should never mix.

'And since you brought up Sinai, wasn't it at Sinai that Yahweh also said, "Thou shalt not steal and thou shalt not kill?" So I would be grateful if you would return the scalpel you have taken to me, its rightful owner, and let Mrs Alphaeus go. I don't want her blood pressure rising any higher. It's not her fault her husband's a tax collector for central government.'

Luke is so talented, so unruffled . . . I could imagine him with a megaphone, cajoling the most hardened terrorist to give his hostages up.

Mrs Alphaeus was amazingly calm, too, well used to being the butt of people's anger. The Romans had recently started taxing fish and grapes, previously VAT exempt, so there was a lot of bad feeling about. 'Let me go, Susannah, please. Why pick on me? What can I do about Roman fiscal policy?'

'You can protest, you can deny your husband his marital rights. That'll soon make him think twice about working for his Roman lords and masters.'

'There aren't a lot of marital rights to deny when you're as pregnant as this,' Mrs Alphaeus quipped. Even Susannah couldn't argue with that, and relaxed her grip slightly. 'And there'd be no marital rights at all to deny if I was dead,' she went on, pressing home her advantage. 'What influence could I wield then? Even tax collectors aren't into necro-philia! Better a live dog who can bark at her husband than a dead lion who can roar no more.'

Yet another proverb, slightly elaborated I fear, but it did the trick, and the futility of her protest dawned on Susannah. Yet still her patriot eyes blazed as she wielded the scalpel dangerously. In a flash Luke realized she needed to withdraw with some honour still intact. He sidled over, all innocent like, and swiftly gave Susannah a swift jab in the kidneys. Immediately she bent double and let Mrs Alphaeus go, and he snatched the scalpel away. The self-defence course gentle Luke had completed to cope with patriot Zealots who gave Gentiles a hard time had clearly come into its own at last.

Mrs Alphaeus cooed over Mrs Zealotes as she lay writhing on the floor, 'I would have done it, I would have done it,' Susannah groaned.

'Of course you would have, dear,' Mrs Alphaeus soothed, mixing a heady concoction of sympathy and death wish. 'We all realize how brave you are, we all respect your devo-tion to Israel's cause. But look, all this confrontation is getting us nowhere. Let's make a pact. I'll do my utmost to deter my little one from following in his father's footsteps at the tax office. You for your part must try to set your little one on the way of peaceful protest rather than bloodshed. I have a dream in which I can see my Matthew and your Simon growing up, playing in the same gang, being great friends! Let's make that dream reality.'

I began to see Mrs Alphaeus in a new light. There was something in the way she drawled over the words 'I have a dream' which reminded me of Martin Luther King. Was she yet another one with this strange relationship with time?

'You really shouldn't have hit Susannah like that, Luke,' I

teased as we rode home. 'Those who live by violence will die by violence.'

'Maybe,' he replied. 'But increasingly I put more and more store by the limited strike option when it comes to resolving Middle Eastern conflict.'

'Watch yourself, Luke! You're beginning to sound like the Yanks,' I warned. Talented, good looking, yet I can be so cutting sometimes.

~ Sunday 7 November ~

I'm laid up with swollen ankles – leaden, I feel as if I'm carrying the world's woes in my womb. To amuse me Dr Luke smuggled in a statue he'd brought back from his recent forays into the twentieth century. 'Who's this supposed to be, then?' I asked.

'You!' he replied, with a broad grin.

I didn't recognize myself. I looked so serious, so thin, so Italian. Not a bit pregnant. 'Why didn't you bring back "Our Lady of the Swollen Ankles?"' I asked Luke.

'Oh, they're not quite ready for that sort of thing yet,' Luke replied. If they're not quite ready for it after two millennia, I guess they never will be.

~ Monday 8 November ~

Ankles not so swollen today. For a break, Luke suggests I shadow him on his rounds. First port of call is a shabby looking house at Cana, a home clearly needing a woman's touch. There was a woman there, lying listlessly on a divan in the corner, her husband and the rest of her household giving her the widest of berths. She was deadly pale, her skin as white as porcelain.

Luke sat for a long time by her bedside, listening, patting her hand, shaking his head in sorrow. As we rode away from Cana, the words streamed from him, words of compassion, words of anger. 'There's so many like her, Miriam, and there's nothing I can do. The birth of her last child went badly wrong, twelve years back, and she's been bleeding ever since, day in, day out. Her strength daily ebbing away, with nothing to replace it in the scraps of food her family leave out for her. I don't know what eats her up more, the anaemia or the isolation the bleeding forces upon her.'

Under our strict law, any woman in her situation is ritually unclean, to be avoided if you don't want to incur Yahweh's misogynistic wrath. Hence her twelve years of solitary confinement, on top of everything else. 'It's not you that's failed her, Luke, it's her family,' I sympathized. 'You prescribed the iron-rich diet, the nightly bottle of Guinness, the vitamin tablets. They were the ones who withheld them from her, throwing her the scraps, treating her no better than a dog. You talked to her, you held her hand, you treated her as human. We Jews have faith enough to move mountains, and yet without your love we are nothing.'

'Miriam, you'd make a great rabbi!' Luke's smile returned, but still he had the look of deep sadness in his eyes.

~ *Tuesday 9 November* ~

Luke's medical roadshow reached Capernaum today. A pallid, emaciated, little boy, huddled shivering in a corner of a house. 'Keep clear of him, he's devil-possessed,' spat the child's father, warning us to keep our distance.

'Not Satan, but epilepsy,' pronounced Luke. As if acting on cue, the child fell over and started shaking, convulsing and foaming at the mouth.

'See how the devil racks him,' the child's father hissed. 'Take this to him,' he urged, handing Luke a leather belt. 'Beat the evil spirit out of him.'

I was aghast as I saw Luke take the belt from the father and move slowly towards the boy. 'Luke, this is barbaric!' I screamed.

But instead of whipping the boy, he cradled his shaking head in his arms, gently prized open the boy's mouth and inserted the belt. 'A bit for between his teeth', Luke explained, 'to stop him biting his tongue off.' Luke stayed beside him until the fit subsided, leaving the boy grey and limp. All eyes in the house were drawn to the pool by the child's side, where he had wet himself, the ultimate humiliation.

The boy's mother stood silently watching throughout. Watching her brute of a husband call down curses on their offspring; watching her child edge towards death; watching Luke bestow the care she was held back from giving. Visibly aching because of her powerlessness, yet watching with a look that was nothing less than sheer love.

~ Wednesday 10 November ~

Still on tour. A friendly bunch of fishermen row us across the lake, bound for Gergesenes. But three miles out from land, at the lake's deepest point, we are caught in a sudden storm. The boat pitches and rolls, up to the sky one minute, plunging down into the depths the next, but the sailors keep calm, well used to Galilee's tricks. They bide their time and energy until the squall passes, and then row frantically for the shore.

'Those who go down to the sea in ships see the works of God and his wonders in the deep.' When the psalmist David penned those words, he didn't mention that sea-sickness and pregnancy sickness conspire together. At one point I felt so awful, I feared I would die. Then I felt so much worse, and feared I wouldn't die.

~ Thursday 11 November ~

I didn't die. To give me a break, Luke whisks me off to London smack in the middle of the 1980s. At 11 o'clock the place proved even more depressing than our depressing medical roadshow, everyone standing still, poppies in their lapels, remembering their war-dead while simultaneously funding arms to fuel further wars. To cheer ourselves up, we go to see another Andrew Lloyd Webber show, *The Phantom of the Opera.*

'I'm not going if it's about me again,' I complain to Luke.

'I don't think it is,' Luke explained. 'It's total fantasy, through and through, starring a brilliant singer called Sarah Brightman as Christine, who embraces a hideous creature to promote music. Pure escapism. And the music is sheer thrill.'

Which it was. Yet the splenetic Phantom, ultimately melted by Christine's love, had the look and sound of Yahweh about him. I shivered, despite the warmth of the theatre. 'Even if I go to see *The Phantom of the Opera*, thou art there, Yahweh,' as David says in Psalm 199. A prophetic guy, my hero.

~ Friday 12 November ~

Sundry patients that poor old Luke can do nothing for. The deaf stay deaf, the blind stay blind, the dumb stay dumb. I can see now why he and Theophilus enjoy the ante-natal clinics so much, with their promise of life and a positive outcome. Even then, they are thwarted by the number of women dying in labour in this primitive land. But at least sometimes is better than never.

~ Saturday 13 November ~

Holed up for the Sabbath in Tiberias, on our return to Nazareth. Even Gentiles deserve a day of rest, but Luke's Sabbath is broken by an urgent request, 'Please come quickly, my daughter, my only daughter is dying.' Considering the seriousness of the mission, I am amazed that Luke positively saunters along, as if he had all the time in the world. I suppose you have all the time in the world when certain failure will be the outcome yet again.

As we stroll along, we are met by the man's servant, with face downcast. 'No need to trouble the doctor further, sir. Your daughter is dead.' As stark as that. No soft soap, no letting down gently. Well, that's that then. We fail with the living. Yahweh help us with the dead.

But Luke surprises me, 'Even so, we'd still like to see her.' We plod on, a call-out turned into a cortège, until we reach the house, and are assailed by the wailing, 'Oi, oi, oi . . .' The mother, the neighbours, chant an incessant litany, a sheer cacophony of grief. 'What's he here for? He's no good when we're alive, let alone when we're dead,' one of them sneers.

With the father beside him, Luke walks through the scathing crowd and pushes them away. Now alone with the father and mother, we are shown to the girl's bed, her death bed. The child's eyes stare vacantly into the heavens as we all gaze at her, in grief-wracked homage. All except Luke. He makes as if to kneel in reverence beside her, but then suddenly lifts her by the shoulders, turns her over so she

83

lies across his knee and then strikes her in the back. Hard.
Three times.

The girl coughs and splutters, her eyes brightening as,
against all the odds, life returns. The parents watch with
silent amazement. Luke is all matter of fact, as if his every
case concluded with a child being brought back to life. 'Give
the girl something to drink,' he commands the mother,
preparing to make our exit. 'Come on, Miriam, we need to
turn in early if we are to set off for Nazareth at dawn.'

As we walked through the no-longer-jeering crowd, the
father's imploring voice rang in my ears, 'My friends, let us
eat and be merry, for this my daughter was dead and is alive
again.'

I gave Luke a well-deserved hug. 'Dr Luke, you're a winner
at last!' Then noticed his countenance was deeply troubled,
and asked, 'Why look so glum after a success like that?'

'I'm just worried about where we go from here, Miriam,'
he replied. 'When you've staged a resurrection, what on earth
can you follow that with?'

~ Wednesday 8 December ~

I gave my parents a card today with 'Happy Hanukkah'
scratched out (you still can't get anything but). Instead I'd
written, 'Smile, I'm your immaculate conception!' They
were completely bewildered rather than amused, however.
It's a hard life, having God incarnate grow inside you and at
the same time having parents oblivious to the finer points
of Catholic theology.

~ Monday 20 December ~

Joe, Dr Luke and I leave Nazareth, bound by donkey for

84

Bethlehem. The local louts are on leave from their military service for Hanukkah, and, like everyone else, are already fed up with the festivities and the endless stream of visiting relatives. So eager for any diversion, they turn out to bid us farewell, throwing stones, displaying their immense repertoire of invective, yelling 'Adulteress!' at me, 'Gentile Dog!' at Luke and 'Cuckold!' at Joe. Nice of them to organize a send-off.

~ Tuesday 21 December ~

It was no summer progress. A cold coming we had of it, at this time of the year; just the worst time of the year to take a journey, and specially a long journey. The ways deep, the weather sharp, the days short, the sun farthest off in *solstitio brumali*, the very dead of winter. And the ass queues stretch back for miles . . .

~ Wednesday 22 December ~

I whispered yesterday's words to Lancelot Andrewes. He was Bishop of Winchester in 1622 and was a bit pushed for something to say in his Christmas Day sermon – he'd preached a fair few before, and had run out of ideas.

Would you believe the audacity of the man? He never had the decency to attribute his source. There he was in the cathedral pulpit, arms gesticulating, looking as if butter wouldn't melt in his mouth, with the congregation lapping up every flourish, when all the time he was plagiarizing *my* prose poetry. I really do think bishops should set a better example.

And not only that, he switched subjects. Instead of retaining some vestige of decency, and using my words to describe me, he rabbits on about the three kings. Some cold coming they had of it, with their thermal robes and heated camel seats and five star accommodation. And because they were on camels rather than asses, he's forced to leave out the best line in the piece, about the ass queue. I ask you, what a liberty!

~ Thursday 23 December ~

And another fall-out from Andrewes' deceit was that T. S. Eliot then cribbed his words (which were mine to start with) to write his infamous poem, 'Journey of the Magi'. It's been read out at every pseudo-intellectual trendy carol service ever since, and is as incomprehensible as Yahweh himself. But set down this, set down this: Have I been led all this way for people to write poems about me which make no sense at all, or to achieve something more tangible?

~ Friday 24 December ~

I'm going to get Luke to ring up *Weekend Watchdog* and complain about that travel agents in Nazareth. Their package promised us five star accommodation in Bethlehem, but then when we got here we found all the hotels quadruple-booked, so we've ended up in this smelly stable, definitely one star judging from the single celestial light shining overhead.

And it's so crowded, what with Joseph and Luke and me, extra heavy with child, as well as all the animals. Not to mention the 6,289 portrait painters with brushes poised, ready to capture the big moment. Luke has just returned from one of his trips to London. Visiting the Houses of Parliament, he picked up a few tips on how to be a spin doctor as well as a medical doctor. So, despite the crowd, at least Luke has got all the artists under control, making sure only the most delicate of poses reaches the final canvas.

~ Sunday 26 December ~

What a day yesterday proved! Trust me to give birth on the dreaded Sabbath. I'll never forget the pain, the searing intense pain, as if my whole body was being torn apart. At the start of things, in his rather jolly annunciation, my friend the lisping angel never even hinted about all this agony.

As the contractions did their worst, I cried out, 'I am poured out like water, and all my bones are out of joint: my heart also, in the midst of my body, is even like melting wax.'

'If you don't mind, Miriam, we'll omit Psalm 22,' Yahweh came in. 'It's one of the few good ones, and I was saving it up for Good Friday.'

'But my Lord, the pain, the terrible pain. I'd rather be crucified than go through all this!' I countered.

'Who says it isn't both/and rather than either/or,' he quipped, his usual taciturn self.

'I can see it, I can see it,' Luke interrupted our cosy dialogue.

'What, the baby's head?' I asked, panting for breath.

'No,' said Luke, looking serious.

'Oh Yahweh, don't let it be a breech birth, after all this!' I prayed.

'No, it's not a head, it's a halo,' Luke explained, his furrowed brow clearing. 'Cheer up, where there's a halo, there'll be a head not far behind.'

Then came the worst pain of the lot. But all of a sudden,

there he was, a tiny weenie baby wriggling in the straw, looking so beautiful yet so vulnerable, so very vulnerable. Kneeling before the little mite, Luke carefully, reverently, picked him up as if he was handling the most precious treasure since creation's dawn and laid him at my breast. His little lips gently nuzzled as the Lord of the heavens took his first drink on earth.

Tears ran like a river down my face. I looked around. Everyone and everything was so still, angels in mid-flight, shepherds with mouths agape, the magi (yes, they did coincide with the shepherds) like statues on bended knee, the artists with brushes poised in mid air: All frozen for a moment of eternity as the immensity of it all dawned.

And then the whole scene sprang back to life again, only the light brighter, the colours richer, the textures deeper, the sounds musical perfection. I could hear the angels trilling the Hallelujah Chorus from Handel's *Messiah*. Though exhausted, I felt like standing because I felt so proud. So deeply proud that my eyes were pools of water and my voice froze in my throat.

When all was calm, I whispered to my tender doctor, 'Luke, that halo, do you think we'll be able to turn it off at night?'

'Miriam,' Luke replied, his face totally dead-pan, 'With this child you will never, ever sleep.' Just the sort of thing Yahweh would have said. I'll have to watch Luke: Yahweh's taciturnity is obviously contagious.

~ Northumbrian Sequence IV ~

Let in the wind
Let in the rain
Let in the moors tonight,

The storm beats on my window-pane,
Night stands at my bed-foot,
Let in the fear,

Let in the pain,
Let in the trees that toss and groan,
Let in the north tonight.

Let in the nameless formless power
That beats upon my door,
Let in the ice, let in the snow,
The banshee howling on the moor,
The bracken-bush on the bleak hillside,
Let in the dead tonight

The whistling ghost behind the dyke,
The dead that rot in mire,
Let in the thronging ancestors
The unfulfilled desire,
Let in the wraith of the dead earl,
Let in the dead tonight.

Let in the cold,
Let in the wet,
Let in the loneliness,
Let in the quick,
Let in the dead,
Let in the unpeopled skies.

Oh how can virgin fingers weave
A covering for the void,
How can my fearful heart conceive
Gigantic solitude?
How can a house so small contain
A company so great?

Let in the dark,
Let in the dead,
Let in your love tonight.

Let in the snow that numbs the grave,
Let in the acorn-tree,
The mountain stream and mountain stone,
Let in the bitter sea.

Fearful is my virgin heart
And frail my virgin form,
And must I then take pity on
The raging of the storm
That rose up from the great abyss
Before the earth was made,
That pours the stars in cataracts
And shakes this violent world?

Let in the fire,
Let in the power,
Let in the invading might.

Gentle must my fingers be
And pitiful my heart
Since I must bind in human form
A living power so great,
A living impulse great and wild
That cries about my house
With all the violence of desire
Desiring this my peace.

Pitiful my heart must hold
The lonely stars at rest,
Have pity on the raven's cry
The torrent and the eagle's wing,
The icy water of the tarn
And on the biting blast.

Let in the wound,
Let in the pain,
Let in your child tonight.

Kathleen Raine,
(Praying with the English Poets, Triangle, 1990)